Frankenbug

Frankenbug

Steven Cousins

Holiday House / New York

Copyright © 2000 by Steven D. Cousins
All Rights Reserved
Printed in the United States of America
www.holidayhouse.com
First Edition

Library of Congress Cataloging-in-Publication Data
Cousins, Steven.
Frankenbug / by Steven Cousins.
p.   cm.
Summary: Inspired by the movie Frankenstein,
bug-lover Adam Cricklestein decides
to create a monster bug that will protect him
from the school bully, Jeb McCallister.
ISBN 0-8234-1496-5 (hardcover)
[1. Insects—Fiction. 2. Bullies—Fiction. 3. Schools—Fiction.
4. Interpersonal relations—Fiction.] I. Title.
PZ7.C83185 Fr 2000   00-035104
[Fic]—dc21

For Emily

Frankenbug

chapter

All the kids in my class think I'm weird.

They're right.

My name is Adam Cricklestein, which is a little weird to begin with, but they call me things like Adam Ant, Cricketman, or sometimes just Buzz. Not because I have a buzz haircut, but because I'm a bug freak. Bugs are my life. My room is full of them. Some I keep in jars and old fish tanks, like the ones that bite or sting or make slime trails, but most I just let crawl and fly around on their own. It's okay with my mom, except that I won't let her vacuum my floor anymore. Not since she accidentally sucked up a rare earwig named Earl. Luckily he survived the ride into the dust bag. In fact, when I finally found him in there he seemed to be enjoying himself. All those crumbs and dust balls—it must have been paradise.

Anyway, my mom lets me get away with this because she's at work all day, my dad's always traveling on business, and I don't have any brothers or sisters or pets. Dogs or cats are too much like humans. But bugs—they're different. What other living creatures have greenish-yellow blood, six legs, and skeletons on the outside instead of the inside? None that I know of. Unless they're aliens.

I caught my first grasshopper when I was nine months old. I was just crawling around in my backyard one morning and grabbed it with my hand. I tried to eat it but it jumped out of my mouth just in time. According to my mom, the June bug I caught the next day wasn't so lucky.

I started my insect zoo when I was three. The first summer all I had were easy ones like roly-polies, ladybugs, and woolly-bear caterpillars. By the time I was five I had almost every kind of bug in our town, even a buffalo treehopper, a hickory horned devil, and a walkingstick. I charged the neighborhood kids five cents for admission. They could stay for fifteen minutes, and if they got pinched, bitten, or stung, they got a refund. Sally-Jo Baxter was the only kid who got pinched *and* bitten, but it was partly her fault because she came to my zoo barefoot. Anyway, I gave her a refund *and* I bought her a cherry popsicle from the popsicle man that afternoon.

I caught some of the bugs in my zoo in my backyard, which has an elm, a crab apple, and a sycamore tree, honeysuckle bushes all around the fence, and an old, overgrown garden full of milkweed, thistle, ragwort, and nettles that I planted myself. I call it the Caterpillar Café. But most of the bugs I found in the woods near my house.

When I was six I gave up on zoos and started doing experiments instead. The first one was just putting bugs together in a cage and watching them fight. It works best with field crickets and stag beetles. The crickets whip each other with their feelers and butt each other on the head like goats. Stag beetle fights are even better. They pick each other up with their moose-antler mandibles and do body slams on each other. They fight best when there's a girl beetle around. Just like some guys I know at school.

Another experiment I did was with bumblebees. They're a little dangerous to work with, so the first thing I did was invent a secret formula to make them fall asleep. (I can't say what was in it, but all the ingredients came from the kitchen cabinet and the supply shelf in the basement.) Then, after the bees were knocked out, I operated on them one by one and took out their stingers. A few of the bigger ones woke up during the operation and stung me, but I had a dish of baking soda paste all ready for emergencies. It works a lot better than mud, which is what I used to use.

Anyway, after I finished the operation I carried all my bumblebees around the neighborhood in my hand. Most of the kids ran away screaming, but a few hung around and asked me how I did it. I said it's none of their beeswax.

I like summers best. Every afternoon I go to the insect room of the museum to help Mr. Simmons, the curator. The insect room is just about my favorite place in the world. It's as big as a classroom, with five long aisles of glass-topped, wooden display cases that smell like paradichlorobenzene crystals. They smell like mothballs. They're not for killing moths, though. They're to keep the museum beetles from eating up all the specimens.

Mr. Simmons's desk is in the corner. He's an entomologist, which is a scientist who studies bugs for a living. He doesn't make a big deal about it, though—that he's a real scientist—and he sure doesn't dress up like one, either. Half the time, especially on weekends, you could easily mistake him for a cowboy or a lumberjack.

Mr. Simmons always tells me that you don't need to be a real scientist to make great discoveries, especially with bugs because there's so much still unknown about them. He gives me lots of advice on my experiments, and he likes to tell me stories about bug-hunting expeditions he's taken to faraway places like New Caledonia, Mount Kinabalu, and the Spice Islands. He has so many adventures to tell that sometimes I forget he's an entomologist. Sometimes he does too. But he always gets his bug in the end.

Mr. Simmons says he was just like me when he was a kid and that I can have his job someday. Meanwhile he lets me label jars and mount specimens, and sometimes he takes me to the woods to find new bugs for the museum collection. A few of the bugs in the display cases I even caught myself, like the alfalfa looper, the twelve-spotted cucumber beetle, and the silver-washed fritillary.

To tell you the truth, I'd rather be hunting bugs or doing experiments than swimming at the pool. Actually I didn't used to mind going to the pool because it was a good place to catch dragonfly nymphs and mosquito wrigglers. But then someone complained and they increased the chlorine.

chapter

2

Now you can see why kids think I'm weird. But mostly they don't bother me—except for one, that is. His name is Jeb McCallister, and he's the class bully. Some girls like him because he's strong and good at sports, but most of the guys are afraid of him.

Jeb makes spitballs with gum instead of paper. He can hit almost any target, even the intercom speaker on the wall or somebody's head in the front row (which isn't bad from the back row, where he always sits). He once stuck Janice Auftenberg's ponytail to the back of her chair with a wad of about five pieces. When she got up to answer a math problem it stretched all the way to the black-board.

Jeb also sets off Black Cats in the toilet and slings meatballs with his spoon in the cafeteria. He even swipes baseball cards from the drugstore, the kind with the big slab · of bubble gum inside. He just sticks the pack into his back pocket when nobody's looking and walks out. Once he got caught, but nothing bad happened to him because his dad is the chief of police. Jeb says that if we ever tell on him, his dad'll throw us in jail. That doesn't make any sense, but we don't tell on him anyway.

Jeb picks on a lot of kids in our class, but me especially. He calls me Bugbrain. His favorite thing to say to me is, "Quit buggin' me, Bugbrain!" or "Buzz off, Bugbrain!" Then he cracks up at how clever he is.

Jeb's got this thing about my bugs. Why I don't know, but whenever he wants to get me, he gets my bugs. Usually he tortures them first, ripping their wings or snapping their legs, then he squashes them with his foot. I'm not sure which he likes better, actually torturing and squashing them, or watching me watch him do it.

One summer when I was making a map of the slime trails on my front porch Jeb made me pick one of the trails and eat the slug at the end of it. I picked the skinniest trail, but unfortunately the slug at the end wasn't a baby. Actually they're not so bad, as long as you don't chew. I didn't get sick or anything, but I did feel a little sluggish for a while.

Another summer I was giving a cricket concert to some kids on my front yard at night with six jars of crickets and a flashlight. Jeb came over and asked why he hadn't been invited. I said I just forgot. He said too bad and broke the legs of the crickets so they couldn't chirp. He got it wrong, of course, but it didn't matter. When a few of the crickets started up again, he just crushed them all with his foot.

About the worst thing Jeb ever did happened last fall, on the first day of fifth grade. The night before, I'd sugared the trunk of the elm tree as usual with my special fizz-blend of mashed bananas, brown sugar, and root beer, and I sneaked out of my bedroom window with my flashlight for one last look. There were a couple of beetles on the sugar. I was just about to reach up and get them, but then I noticed something else clinging on the bark that I'd never seen before, something strange and beautiful with long, pale-green wings. It was a moon moth.

I turned off my flashlight and stood there, watching him. He was just shimmering there in the darkness like some kind of ghost. After a while I raised my net as carefully as I could. The moon moth didn't try to fly away. He didn't even know he was being caught.

School started the next day, and I took the moon moth to show my classmates. They all loved him, except for one. Jeb was waiting for me halfway home from school.

"Hand it over, Bugbrain," he said, chewing his gum.

I shook my head. "Uh-uh."

"Don't you have ears, man? I said hand it over!" Jeb yanked the cage from my hands and dashed toward his house, whooping and tossing the cage in the air.

I chased him of course, but I wondered why Jeb didn't just squash him right away. As soon as I got to his yard I found out.

"Time for some target practice!" he yelled. He turned up the garden hose all the way, but kept the nozzle shut tight. Then he put the moth cage down on the ground, flipped open the top, and took aim with both hands.

"NOOOOO!" I shouted as Jeb followed the moon moth with the dripping nozzle. But it was too late. As soon as the moth flew up about ten feet, Jeb twisted the nozzle and blasted him out of the air.

"Pretty good shot, huh, Bugbrain?" he sneered.

The moon moth twitched on the ground a few seconds, then fluttered back up. Jeb squeezed one eye shut as he followed its zigzagging path.

I sprang over to block him, but Jeb swung the nozzle straight at my face.

"Don't try it!" he warned, then whipped the nozzle back up to the sky. "Ready . . . Aim . . . FIRE!"

The moth dropped to the ground and I ran to it, but Jeb beat me there. He grabbed my shoulder and heaved me down, popping two buttons off my shirt. For a second I couldn't suck in any air, but Jeb pointed the hose anyway. The water gushed hard, and Jeb kept spraying until my clothes were all soaked through. Then he flung down the hose and turned off the spigot.

"Now beat it, Bugbrain," Jeb hollered from the front porch, "before my dad comes home and arrests you for trespassing!"

I got up dripping wet and went to the moon moth lying by the curb. The green dust was all washed off his wings, and he couldn't fly anymore. He died in my room the next day.

After that I knew I had to do something about Jeb. But what? He was bigger than me—a lot bigger. Even if I learned karate he could probably still beat me up. And like I said, Jeb always went for my bugs first, not me. If only *they* could fight back, I thought, if only *they* could teach the bully a lesson.

A few weeks later I tried walking around the neighborhood with some cicadas in a jar. I hid some hornets under a piece of cardboard in the bottom. I figured that when Jeb dumped the cicadas out to smash them, the hornets would fly out and attack him.

But even Jeb wasn't that dumb. He just shook the jar and made the hornets burning mad. They buzzed up hard against the glass and stung the poor cicadas about five times each. Luckily they weren't dead, just paralyzed for a few days. After that they flew away.

So much for the hornets-in-the-jar trick.

I was beginning to see that my only hope of getting a bug to attack Jeb would be to train him that way. After all, bugs can learn too. Ants are pretty good at mazes and I once taught some yellow cabbage butterflies to land on my hand. But training a bug to attack Jeb would be much harder than that. And it would take more than an ant or a butterfly to get the job done.

I was thinking about this one day when I had an idea. It was a drizzly Saturday in October, and I was in the family room watching *Frankenstein* on television. It's an old movie, in black and white, and I'd seen it before. But this time was different. I had the feeling the movie was telling me something, like some kind of hidden message no one else could understand. I watched how Dr. Frankenstein made his monster from the parts of dead bodies. How he stitched them together in his laboratory and brought them to life, late on a stormy, thundering night.

"It's moving! It's alive!" shrieked Dr. Frankenstein through the smoke and snapping sparks, and that's when it came to me, like one of those sparks jumping to my brain: if Dr. Frankenstein could make his own monster, why couldn't I?

Not out of human parts, of course, but out of bug parts. A monster bug that I would build with my very own hands and bring to life in my very own room. A monster bug fierce and powerful enough to protect me from Jeb McCallister, but small enough not to attract too much attention. Yes—I would create a monster! And in the next moment, before he'd even come into being, I gave my monster his name:

Frankenbug.

chapter

3

I knew I had to start with the basics. That's
what my teacher Mr. Avery always said: "It's
the *basics*, people, you have to start with the
basics!" Mainly he was talking about math
problems, not making monster bugs, but
I knew it still applied. Even Dr. Frankenstein had to study a lot before he started his
monster, mostly chemistry, physiology, and
anatomy. Luckily insect bodies weren't as
complicated as human ones.

The first thing I did was check out some
insect books from the public library. Not the
kind I used to read in second or third grade,
the ones with big letters and bright pictures

like *Backyard Bug Safari, You Can Catch a Snail,* or *Creepy Crawlies A to Z.* Instead I checked out the thick kind with small letters like *Outline of Entomology, Principles of Insect Biology,* and *Morphology of the Insect Abdomen.* The librarian gave me a curious look when I brought them up to the checkout desk.

"Need a bag for those?" she asked.

"Yes, please," I answered.

"Are you working on a project for school?"

"No, I finished my bug unit in second grade. This is for some research I'm doing on my own."

The librarian smiled a little. "Well, it looks pretty complicated—I'll say that much," she said as she stamped the due date into my books.

I nodded quietly. If she only knew.

She stacked up the books and rested her hands on top of them for a moment. "My son Jeffrey used to love bugs when he was your age," she said, gazing off into the aisles. "He used to catch June beetles in the summer— they were his absolute favorite. Did you ever try catching any of those?"

"Hm-mmm," I nodded. I was about to tell her how I caught one and ate it when I was only nine months old, but I didn't want to brag.

"They bump into my window screen a lot," I said. "Sometimes when I lift it open at night they fly right into my room."

"Oh, they do do that, don't they?" said the librarian with a chuckle. "So that's how you usually catch them?"

"Um . . . not usually. Because if I open my screen too long, everything else in my room flies out."

The librarian kept smiling but just stared at me. "Well, good luck to you in your research," she said after a long moment.

"Thank you," I replied.

As soon as I got home I started studying. I propped up the thickest book, *Principles of Insect Biology,* on my lap, opened it to the middle, and began reading.

In Malpighian tubules the basal lamella prevents particles from clogging the deep parallel infolds of the basal plasma membrane, though in some species this fibrous matrix remains permeable to large proteins such as horseradish peroxidase.

At least I knew what horseradish was.

I looked over at the figure on the opposite page. According to the caption, it was the cross-sectional view of a whirligig's Malpighian tubule. To me it looked more like a butter crunch doughnut.

Maybe I should start from chapter one, I thought, on anatomy.

Actually I already knew quite a bit about anatomy, for example how the three main parts—head, thorax, abdomen—fit together. But to build a monster bug that really came to life, that really crawled and buzzed and attacked bullies, I had to learn a lot more, about parts I'd never heard of, like the ocelli, lacinia, paraglossa, pulvilli, and ovarioles. For some reason a lot of the parts sounded like Italian food.

Three nights later, lying on my bed with *Principles of Insect Biology,* I had my first feelings of doubt. I'd made it through anatomy and was just starting to study digestion. I flipped ahead to see how many pages were left in the chapter, looking for parts I could skip, and suddenly I saw it again—the cross-sectional view of a whirligig's Malpighian tubule. Only now, instead of a doughnut, it looked like a life preserver. I was sinking, I had to admit—I was in too deep.

Who was I kidding? A boy my age was supposed to be playing football or watching TV. Instead I was making a monster bug. From scratch.

I let *Principles of Insect Biology* slide off my lap. I picked up my homework folder and got out my spelling list for that week. The words were a lot easier than "Malpighian tubule." I gazed at them.

1. grapefruit (My dad and I don't need sugar, but my mom does.)
2. Wednesday (the day after tomorrow)
3. caterpillar (Clyde the hawkmoth caterpillar, munching willow leaves up on my shelf)
4. peculiar (me)

5. digestion (In bugs, it takes place in the foregut, midgut, and hindgut.)
6. muscular (not me)
7. nerve (one of the hardest things to hook up in a homemade monster bug)
8. broccoli (At least it's not lima beans.)
9. loyalty (Would I get it from Frankenbug?)
10. mysterious (one of my favorite things)
11. nuisance (too nice a word for Jeb McCallister)
12. horrible (That's more like it.)

There were ten or so more words, but I'd seen enough. Crazy or not—making a monster bug was my last hope to fight back. A lot of people thought Dr. Frankenstein was crazy too, but he didn't let that stop him. Besides, I was starting to go crazy by not doing anything at all about Jeb.

To really succeed, though, maybe I'd need some help. And there was only one person who knew enough about insects and was just crazy enough to believe my experiment might work: Mr. Simmons. In fact, Mr. Simmons was used to weird experiments, the kind that other people don't really think have a chance. He'd done a few of those himself. I know, because he let me be his assistant.

Mr. Simmons is trying to prove a theory that moths communicate not just by scent but also by electromagnetic waves, kind of like the signals radios and TVs use. Not too many people think he's right, though. In fact, I'm the only one. Mr. Simmons even lost his job at the university because the other professors didn't believe him.

But he doesn't mind. The first thing he did after changing jobs was build a strange-looking machine for picking up moth signals. We call it the "moth meter," and it has colored knobs and looping wires and a set of twirling rabbit-ear antennae on top. So far Mr. Simmons hasn't picked up any signals (except a New York Mets game and a weather report from Rio de Janeiro), but he says that's just because he hasn't found the right kind of moth yet. Whenever he gets a chance, he takes off on expeditions in his old VW Beetle to find new ones to test on his machine.

Meanwhile the moth meter just sits in the corner of the insect room, gathering dust. It's been there so long that last summer a family of brown-banded cockroaches moved in and made a home inside it. They hardly ever come out, which means they're feeding on the soft parts of the machine, just like they do with TVs. I told Mr. Simmons I'd be happy to get them out of there, but he shook his head.

"It's all right," he said. "Now when the experiment doesn't work, we can just say there's a bug in the machine."

So Mr. Simmons was definitely used to odd experiments, but the more I thought about it, the more I thought this plan of mine might be strange even for him. After all, I wasn't just listening for moth signals, I was creating a new life-form—a monster no less—and Mr. Simmons might think that was risky or something.

Come to think of it, it *was* kind of risky.

Once I created the monster, how did I really know what he would do? What if he attacked not just bullies but innocent people too, or turned into some kind of mutant species that threatened the whole world? What would my parents think?

No, I had to do it alone—I had to keep my project a secret from everybody. It might be dangerous but, after all, the creature was still just a bug. If worse came to worse, I could always just squash it with my foot.

chapter

4

I tried to act normal at home. The only thing my mom noticed was that I was going to bed earlier. She thought it was because I was growing up so fast and needed more sleep. She was wrong. I was hard at work under the covers, drawing sketches of my monster by the light of my flashlight.

Night after night I worked, trying to remember all the things a bug needs to do to survive: fly, feed, and fight enemies. For most bugs the enemies are other bugs, birds, toads, or snakes. But for Frankenbug, in the habitat of my town, there was only one real enemy: Jeb McCallister.

That meant my monster would have to be a fearless carnivore with powerful weapons. I planned on a stinger at least one inch long and sharp enough to go through blue jeans. I also needed strong jaws for biting, heavy pincers for crushing, and a long proboscis for sucking. Not flower nectar, either.

My monster would have to be big to carry all those weapons, but he couldn't be as big as, say, Spider-man, because his exoskeleton would be too heavy to fly around in. Seven inches was the biggest I could make him, or eight inches if you count the stinger.

At that size, of course, camouflage was out of the question. Frankenbug couldn't exactly imitate a broken twig or a shriveled leaf—not to mention thorns or bird droppings. So instead of using camouflage, I had to make him look as dangerous as possible.

With the bugs in my town, that wasn't going to be easy. After all, what kind of a monster could I make with bagworms, June bugs, or daddy longlegs? I needed the giants and the killers of the insect world. And I had a way of getting them.

On his bookshelf at the museum Mr. Simmons kept a big mail-order catalog of bug specimens from all over the world. Sometimes he let me help him fill out orders for the collection. So I already knew what to do.

Once I'd finished sketching my monster, I borrowed the catalog from Mr. Simmons and took it home. There were thousands of bugs to choose from, each with its own picture and description. But most were too small to make a monster with. I soon realized that the biggest and most ferocious bugs of all lived in the tropical rain forest. Those were the bugs for me. I studied their pictures with a magnifying glass and a ruler, looking for the parts that best fit the shape of my monster as I imagined him.

Finally, after three long nights of choosing, I had my list:

1. A goliath beetle of Cameroon, West Africa, for its six-inch body and heavy armor plating.
2. A devil's flower praying mantis of the African Congo, for its head—to give Frankenbug the brain of a hunter.

3. A vampire moth of Malaysia, for its barbed proboscis—strong enough to prick the skin of a water buffalo.
4. A black bulldog ant of Tasmania, one of the most powerful ants in the world, for its jaw muscles.
5. A doodlebug of Amazonia, for its saw-toothed, meat-grinder mandibles.
6. A petalura dragonfly of Australia, for its seven-inch double wings that beat like propellers.
7. An emperor scorpion of Ghana, West Africa, for its massive three-inch pincers and stinger as sharp as a stiletto.
8. A hissing cockroach of Madagascar, for its hairy feelers underneath the abdomen, called cerci, that pick up vibrations in the air and warn of approaching enemies.
9. A death's head cicada of Papua, New Guinea, for its tymbal organs that roar like a fighter bomber and can be heard over a quarter mile away.
10. A giant wetapunga cricket of New Zealand, for its eight-inch, spiky back

legs that are strong enough for karate kicks.

I really wanted to order a thirteen-inch Borneo walkingstick, too, but I couldn't figure out how to use any of his parts. They were just too twiggy.

I filled in the blanks on the order form and signed it Adam Cricklestein, Ph.D. That's how Mr. Simmons always signed it, and I had to make it look official. Then I mailed it in. Ten specimens in all, and it was going to cost me a whole year's worth of saved-up allowance.

Two weeks later the box was sitting on the front doorstep when I got home from school. It had the words PRESERVED INSECTS FOR SCIENTIFIC STUDY written in black stencils above my name. I took the box into my room, cut through the rough twine, and looked inside.

The bugs were big, some even bigger than my hand, and they were beautiful. They came in jars of alcohol, but their colors gleamed like they were still alive, all the colors they needed for hiding in the jungle: the dark green of moss and fern, the reddish brown of tree bark, the yellow specks of light where the sun pokes through the leaves.

The bugs in those jars weren't really dead, I told myself. They were just waiting. Waiting to wake up in a new body, and to crawl and fly and go on the hunt once more. I was sure they'd rather be doing that than sitting in some dusty old museum display case. I thought of it as one last metamorphosis for them, except for one thing: I, Adam Cricklestein, was in charge instead of nature.

It was time to begin my creation.

chapter

5

My first task was to cut off the parts I needed from each specimen. I used my dissecting knife, tweezers, and a magnifying glass. Compared to the book, it wasn't easy to see where one part ended and another began, especially the muscles and nerves and blood vessels. Luckily insect blood just oozes around instead of flows, so not too much leaked out.

After three nights of cutting I was ready to stitch the parts together. This was going to be harder than it was for Dr. Frankenstein. One reason he made his monster eight feet tall was so the parts would be big and easy to work with. Frankenbug was only eight inches long, and some of his parts were smaller than my fingernail.

Sewing thread was obviously too thick. I thought of using the silk of an old cecropia cocoon in my drawer, but I couldn't untangle it. Then I remembered spider silk. It's thin but strong, and would dissolve in a month or so, after the parts of my creature had grown together.

I went to the woods early in the morning to look for webs. That's when the orb weavers start spinning, and I needed to be there to get the bridge lines, the long strands they stretch from branch to branch to hang the rest of the web on. Bridge lines aren't sticky like the others, and they're so strong you can pull them back like a bowstring. I found a few and rolled them up on a twig. Then I went back and borrowed the smallest needle from my mom's sewing kit, threaded it, and waited for night to come.

We had macaroni and cheese for dinner, but I only ate a few bites. I went to bed early. Finally the light under my door went out, and I heard my mom go upstairs. It was time to start.

I switched on the lamp on my desk. That became my operating table. Out of my top drawer I got a stone-carved scarab beetle that my dad brought me back from Egypt and propped it up against the bookend. To the ancient Egyptians, the scarab was a symbol of life—just what I needed.

Then I got the monster parts out of my bottom drawer. I kept them all in separate jars, each with its own label: wings, cerci, tymbal organs, mandibles, pincers, etc.

I started with the body of the goliath beetle and sewed on the big, triangular head of the devil's flower praying mantis. The devil's flower is a killer, but a patient one. He's camouflaged like an orchid and sits alone on the petals waiting for a bug to come by for a sip of nectar. Then he lashes out like lightning with his spiked front legs, so fierce and deadly that in China they've named a style of kung fu after him.

I needed Frankenbug to be patient, too, so I thought this brain was perfect. I wasn't so sure about the color, though. Of the head I mean. The orchid this mantis lived on must have been purple with orange stripes.

Too bad they didn't let you pick the colors on the order form.

Next it was time to put on the weapons. I started with the razor-sharp doodlebug mandibles. Doodlebugs are much more dangerous than they sound. They dig funnel-holes in the sand and wait at the bottom, until their victim wanders by and tumbles down in an avalanche. Then it's all over.

On top of the doodlebug mandibles I fastened the jaw muscles of the black bulldog ant. The bite of this ant is so powerful that people have been killed by it. But that's not the only reason they call him a bulldog. The other is that he jumps up on his victims and doesn't let go.

In between the mandibles I hooked on the proboscis of the vampire moth, which is like a long, coiled spear with barbs on the tip. That was enough for the creature's mouth. It was starting to look like a Swiss army knife.

Next I sewed on the scorpion pincers and tail. Scorpions aren't insects, they're arachnids like spiders, and I wasn't sure if mixing arachnid parts with insect parts was going to work. But I had to try. Frankenbug needed them if he was going to do his job.

I took the venom out, though. It's in little sacs at the end of the tail. I didn't want Frankenbug to actually kill Jeb, just scare him out of his skin.

Once all the weapons were on I attached the hind legs of the giant wetapunga, which were easy to sew because the extensor muscles were so bulgy, and then the wings of the petalura dragonfly. There were four wings in all, two on each side, and with those Frankenbug would be able to fly thirty-five miles an hour, maybe forty.

I fixed the wings so Frankenbug could fold them straight back over his body while he was resting, which dragonflies can't do. They still stuck out from underneath his wing cases, though. It looked kind of like his shirttails weren't tucked in.

Next I put on the cockroach cerci and the tymbal organs of the death's head cicada. Those parts were too small to sew, so I used spittlebug spit to stick them on. I had a whole jar of it up on my shelf, left over from another experiment.

Frankenbug was going to need antennae, too. Not for scenting out a mate, of course, but for smelling his enemy. I could've used the antennae of the vampire moth or the giant wetapunga, but then I thought of the moon moth that Jeb killed. I still had him. The moon moth's antennae can smell the farthest of any bug in the world—more than six miles. And the way I figured it, my moon moth already knew what the enemy smelled like.

I worked on Frankenbug every night for three weeks straight. I didn't even bother to go trick-or-treating on Halloween. Later and later I worked, sometimes past midnight.

Finally, late one night in mid-November, I finished stitching. I sat back in my chair and beheld my creation under the narrow funnel of light.

He looked a little front-heavy, but all the parts fit together and you couldn't even see the stitches unless you looked close. He had a purple-and-orange striped head with feathery green antennae, a maroon-and-white striped thorax, glossy black pincers (which reminded me of boxing gloves), and a glossy black tail. His wing cases were candy-apple red, and the wings underneath were translucent blue with pink and gold sparkles.

All in all, he was a bit too colorful for a monster. In fact, if there were such a thing as a bug of paradise, he would be it. But he did have the shape of a monster, with his googly eyes and dagger-shaped fangs and gigantic pincers. He'd act like one too, once he came to life.

That was the last problem. Dr. Frankenstein had to bring to life a whole human being. Compared to that I had it easy. But how? How could I give Frankenbug the spark of life?

I checked out *Frankenstein* from the public library. (I was a little worried that the librarian might remember me and put two and two together, but luckily she wasn't there.) In chapter four Dr. Frankenstein talks about the "instruments of life," but he keeps them a secret because he doesn't want anyone else to make such a horrible mistake. I could see his point, but somebody found out what he did anyway and wrote it in the appendix. Of the book I mean. He used a giant battery.

That might work for my monster too. The first thing I did was get a flashlight battery and wire it to Frankenbug's hind legs. Nothing happened.

Next I tried hooking it up to his abdomen, just underneath one of the major ganglia. Then his thorax, and finally his head. Maybe a tingle to his brain would do it, I thought. It didn't.

I dug up some 4.5-volt and 9-volt batteries, but that didn't work, either. I even got a paper clip and a piece of copper wire and hooked the creature up to a lemon. But no luck. I didn't get a single twitch.

Then I remembered how in the movie Dr. Frankenstein used lightning to bring his monster to life. He said lightning had a mysterious life force, the same great force that first brought life into the world. That's what I needed too.

The problem was how to get some lightning. Dr. Frankenstein had a lightning rod at the top of a stone watchtower, which I didn't have. He also had a giant machine to hold the lightning and harness its power, which I didn't have. I thought of catching some lightning with a kite like Benjamin Franklin did, but without a machine like Dr. Frankenstein's, even the tiniest zap would fry Frankenbug to a crisp. We almost never had any lightning in November anyway.

Still, I liked the idea of using some kind of natural energy to bring my monster to life. I thought of other kinds like wind, sunshine, and gravity, but none seemed to have the same wallop as lightning.

I opened my science book to look for ideas. There was a big color picture of a dissected bullfrog with all his parts labeled. Mr. Avery hadn't done that experiment yet. Wayne Mitchell said it was because one year Mr. Avery fainted after he sliced open the bullfrog's belly.

It reminded me of the bullfrog I'd used as a nightlight a few summers back. I caught him in the creek in the woods and brought him home to see if Bruce, my pet bombardier beetle, would squirt him with boiling chemicals. Bruce just ran away—but the bullfrog snapped up a lightning bug who'd landed on my bedcovers. Soon I noticed a faint glow in the bullfrog's belly. I fed him another, and then another, and after eating fifteen or so the bullfrog stopped trying to jump around. He was even bright enough to read a book by under the covers.

Lightning bugs. *Lightning* bugs. That was it! If real lightning was too strong, why not use lightning bugs? Their light came from chemicals mixing with air, not from electricity, but still, if regular lightning had that mysterious, life-giving power Dr. Frankenstein talked about, maybe lightning bugs would have it, too.

But now there was another problem: lightning bug season was already over. After school the next day I asked Mr. Simmons if he knew how to get some. I said it was for an experiment, but I didn't say what kind.

Mr. Simmons got back to me a few days later. He had an entomologist friend down South who ran a biological supply house and could loan us some lightning bugs. But we'd have to return them in a day or two. I said that was long enough. And I asked for one hundred of them, all males if possible, since their light is brighter and they're the ones that flash while they're flying. Besides, they had to concentrate on the experiment. The last thing I needed was for them to get distracted by a female lightning bug.

The lightning bugs arrived at Mr. Simmons's office a week later, in a small terrarium filled with dirt and leaves. Mr. Simmons said they were *Photinus carolinus,* a species from the Smoky Mountains.

"Their flash pattern is very different from the lightning bugs around here, *Photinus pyralis,* which give off just a single flash every seven seconds or so," he said. "These guys flash four to nine times in a row, kind of like a Morse code in lights."

"Oh," I said, holding back a smile. That was perfect.

"You can read about them in here," Mr. Simmons added, handing me a pamphlet with the title, "Caring for your *Photinus carolinus.*"

I took the lightning bugs home to get ready for the last part of my experiment. I had only one chance to make it work.

chapter

I'll never forget that night, how slowly the minutes ticked by as I waited to begin, lying on my bed, pacing the floor, looking out my window into the pitch blackness of my backyard. The last thing I needed was spooky weather, but that's what it was, a cold November night with no moon and no stars, and no sound but the wind whisking through my backyard, skittering the dead autumn leaves along the ground.

I closed my curtains. I lay on my bed, tossing up a plastic ball as close to the ceiling as I could without touching it. Finally, around half past eleven, all the lights in the house were out.

I made my room completely dark. Then I pulled the container of lightning bugs out from under my bed, put it in the middle of the floor, and watched as they began to flicker in the darkness, a dim greenish yellow.

From my top shelf I got an old empty fish tank and set it on my desk. That was going to be the energy chamber where my monster would come to life. I'd made a special lid for it, with a lock on the side just in case.

Then I looked at the closet. He was in there, waiting. Now his wait was over. Slowly I pulled open the closet door. It was dark in there, but I knew where the jar was, hidden in the corner. I knelt down, clasped it, and brought the creature out of the closet.

The jar was heavy as I held it up in the darkness. Most of the lightning bugs were flashing now, and by their faint glow I could just make out the creature's pincers and mandibles and huge hind legs behind the glass. For a second I thought I felt his heart beating, but it was only my own.

I set the jar on my desk and unscrewed the lid. Then I reached in, curled my fingers around the creature's abdomen, and slowly lifted him out. I held up my other hand too, just in case any loose parts fell off. But none did. Only the chilly dribble of preserving fluid through my fingers.

Gently I lowered the creature into the energy chamber and stood the stone-carved scarab beetle against the glass in the corner. Then I closed the top.

So far so good.

I glanced over at the lightning bugs. It was time to put them in—but how many would it take?

At first I tried just ten. I waited. The lightning bugs flashed on and off, but nothing happened. I put in ten more. Still nothing. I tried thirty lightning bugs, then fifty, then eighty. The energy chamber was getting crowded, but the creature wasn't responding.

There were only twenty lightning bugs left. They were my last hope. One by one I put them in the chamber. A minute passed. Two minutes. Five minutes.

The creature didn't move.

It was late now, close to midnight, and I was getting tired. But the wind was getting wilder, whipping through the trees and wailing at my window as if something were about to happen. I couldn't give up. One hundred lightning bugs *had* to bring my monster to life.

Then I noticed something. Even though there were a hundred in there, they never flashed at the same time. Only fifteen or so lit up at once. Maybe that wasn't enough. But how could I get a hundred lightning bugs to shine all together?

I sat down at my desk and rested my forehead in my hands. I remembered a story Mr. Simmons once told me about an expedition he'd made to a far-off island in the South Pacific. Canoeing down a river after dark, he'd come upon whole trees, filled with lightning bugs by the thousands, flashing all at once in the black tropical night. On and off, on and off they'd flashed, like giant Christmas trees in the jungle. And I remembered something else Mr. Simmons said, about a trick he'd learned from some forest

44

tribesmen, of calling lightning bugs with a flashlight by imitating their signal. I'd always wanted to try that trick myself, but never did. Now was my chance.

I got my flashlight out of the drawer, held it up to the energy chamber, and started to imitate *Photinus carolinus:* four quick flashes, twelve-second pause; four quick flashes, twelve-second pause.

Nothing happened. I tried again. The lightning bugs just zigzagged around the cage as if I wasn't there.

I couldn't understand it—I was imitating their signal perfectly. I watched them in the darkness, a hundred lightning bugs, blinking at random. Then, suddenly, it hit me: I was just like them—another male! I'd totally forgotten the whole purpose of lightning bug flashes—to find a mate. And I'd forgotten something else too—the female flash pattern is different from the male's!

All I needed, then, was the flash pattern of the female *Photinus carolinus*. But where could I find that? I grabbed the pamphlet, "Caring for your *Photinus carolinus*." Not a single word on flash patterns!

My whole experiment was falling apart because I didn't know the flash pattern of a female lightning bug. I should have ordered at least one. Ninety-nine males would still have been enough. But without at least one female, even a hundred males were useless.

There was only one thing left to do. I crept out of my bedroom and into the kitchen. I got the phone directory, opened to "S", and scanned the names under the tiny light above the stove: Sidwell, Silverman, Simkins, Simmering, Simmons. Simmons, Karl A., 8854 Walnut. That was the one.

I picked up the phone, dialed the number, and listened to it ring—four, five, six times. Then the ringing stopped and there was a pause.

"Hello?" said Mr. Simmons. He sounded groggy.

"Um . . . Mr. Simmons?" I said, muffling my voice with my hand.

"Yes?"

"It's Adam."

"Hello, Adam—what's up?"

"Mr. Simmons, I'm really sorry to be calling so late, but I have a question, and it's kind of an emergency."

"Shoot."

"Well, um . . . I was wondering if you happen to know what the flash pattern of a female *Photinus carolinus* is?"

There was a chuckle on the other end. "What's the matter, did she forget?"

"Oh no. That's not the problem. The problem is, I don't even have a female."

"I know what you mean."

"Huh?"

"Oh, nothing," he said. "Now let's see— that was *Photinus carolinus,* was it?"

"Yes, the same kind we borrowed from your friend."

"Right. Well, I don't know that flash code offhand, but I might have it in a journal somewhere. You need this right now?"

"Uh-huh."

"Okay, hold on just a minute."

"Okay."

I looked out the kitchen window, at the wind howling through the trees, but it was so dark out there that all I could see was my own reflection in the glass. My pale skin and weary eyes reminded me a little of Dr. Frankenstein, but not my messy brown hair and blue flannel shirt.

"Adam?" said Mr. Simmons.

"Yes?"

"I've got it."

"Great!" I whooped, and quickly stared at the ceiling, hoping I hadn't woken up my mom.

"Okay then, here it is: The answering pattern of the female *Photinus carolinus* is two double flashes in a row, with a half-second pause in between. It would go something like this: *flash-flash-pause; flash-flash-pause.*"

"Thank you very much, Mr. Simmons."

"You're welcome, Adam."

"Good-bye."

"Adam?"

"Yes?"

"Are you trying to communicate with them?"

"Uh-huh."

"Okay then—remember to wait two seconds before you answer the males' signal. If you answer too soon or too late, they'll know you're an imposter."

"Okay."

"And once the males start responding, dim your light a little by holding it down at an angle."

"Okay," I said.

"Good luck," said Mr. Simmons.

"Thanks," I said. The phone clicked on the other end, and I slipped back through the shadowy hallway to my bedroom.

I sat down on my chair and held the flashlight about two feet away from the energy chamber. I started pushing the switch on and off with my thumb: *flash-flash-pause; flash-flash-pause.* Then I waited a moment and did it once more: *flash-flash-pause; flash-flash-pause.*

A few of the lightning bugs flew to my side of the energy chamber. But of course, with a hundred of them in there, it could have been just a coincidence. I watched their signal: *flash-pause-flash-pause-flash-pause-flash.* Then I counted to myself—"one, one thousand, two, one thousand"—and answered: *flash-flash-pause; flash-flash-pause.*

The lightning bugs on my side of the chamber flashed again, and now I noticed they were together:

flash-pause-flash-pause-flash-pause-flash;
flash-pause-flash-pause-flash-pause-flash.

I counted two seconds, holding the beam down at an angle, and flashed again. They flashed too, and then I knew for sure. At least ten lightning bugs, hovering on my side of the energy chamber, were with me now, and with one another, making a little globe of light in the darkness as bright—no, even brighter—than my flashlight.

Again I signaled—and again they answered—now twenty of them, thirty, forty:

flash-pause-flash-pause-flash-pause-flash—
flash-flash-pause; flash-flash-pause;
flash-pause-flash-pause-flash-pause-flash—
flash-flash-pause; flash-flash-pause . . .

Now more joined in, and more after that— fifty at least, then sixty, then eighty lightning bugs gathered on my side of the energy chamber:

flash-pause-flash-pause-flash-pause-flash;
flash-pause-flash-pause-flash-pause-flash—

brighter, and brighter, and brighter still—until, suddenly, all of them were with me, all one hundred lightning bugs, all flashing together. Each flash lit up the whole room; each pause made it dark. It was like an orchestra of light, and I was the conductor.

But then I stopped. The lightning bugs quickly lost their rhythm, but their scattered blinking was still enough to see by in the darkness. It was the antennae. The antennae of the creature had moved a little—just a twitch, the smallest twitch—but they'd moved.

Or had they? Maybe I was just seeing things. Maybe the shadows were playing tricks on my eyes. I bent closer, so close that my breath made a cloud on the glass. I peered in at those long, feathery antennae on top of the creature's head. The antennae of the moon moth I'd caught last summer in my backyard, late on a warm and starry night. *Move,* I silently commanded them. *Move.*

And then, amazingly, they did. The antennae moved—just a quiver, like a feather in the breeze—but now I knew for sure it wasn't the shadows. My chest tightened, squeezing out all the air. Slowly I moved around the side of the energy chamber and looked in again, straight into the creature's eyes. They'd always been a dull, muddy brown before—the color of a dead bug's eyes. But not anymore. Now those eyes were a deep, jungle green, as green and deep as the African Congo, and they were glowing.

"It's alive," I whispered. "It's alive!"

chapter

Everything was quiet, even the wind. I just stood there, barely breathing, waiting to see what he would do next. His head swiveled a little in my direction. He was watching me. His eyes had little black pupils in the middle, just like human eyes, so I could tell he was really looking at me. It was creepy.

I reached out and made sure the top of the cage was shut tight. With all the weapons Frankenbug had, no one was safe, not even me.

Then I remembered he had to eat. I went down to the basement and found a cobweb spider in the corner and a silverfish behind the furnace. Not the tastiest meal, I admit, but Frankenbug didn't have to eat it anyway. When I got back to my room he was asleep.

The next morning I took the lightning bugs back to Mr. Simmons on the way to school. He asked if my experiment was a success, and I said yes. I asked him for some food for a praying mantis. He gave me a container of mealworms, and when I got home from school I caught some crickets under the back porch steps.

I'd designed Frankenbug as a predator. He'd eat almost anything that moved—other bugs, of course, but also frogs, lizards, and even mice. But I decided to start him out on bugs and save the vertebrates for later.

Frankenbug was sitting in his cage just where I'd left him. I carefully dropped in some mealworms and waited for the attack. But Frankenbug didn't move. He didn't even look at them. Maybe it was because the mealworms were squirming too slowly to catch his eye. After all, Frankenbug's brain came from a praying mantis, and they only attack moving targets.

So next I tried some crickets. They scurried around all right, and this time Frankenbug did tilt his eyes at them, but he still didn't try to eat them.

Was Frankenbug a fussy eater? That would be hard to understand, because praying mantises aren't fussy at all. But I decided to try out as many kinds of bugs as I could, to see if I could find something he liked.

After school the next day I went to the woods to look for more. But by then it was getting cold outside, and all I could find were some chestnut weevils, aphids, crane flies, ants, and squash bugs. I put them in my lunchbox.

Tramping back across the field, I realized I might have to give up some of my own bugs, too. The first thing I did when I got home was scoop out a spoonful of frozen fleas from my flea jar in the freezer and put them in a dish on the windowsill to thaw. Fleas can come back to life even after a year of being frozen, and sunshine works best.

I checked my room, too. Some bugs I didn't want to give up, like Eddie my pet hedge snail or Clyde, my hawkmoth cater-pillar, who was Eddie's cagemate up on my shelf. And Earl the earwig had already been sucked up by the vacuum cleaner and survived it, so I thought he deserved a break.

I found six ground beetles hibernating in the closet. They were pretty groggy, so I warmed them up under my desk lamp and flicked their antennae until they woke up.

Then I dropped the bugs into the monster's cage one by one, keeping a tally in my notebook of how many there were of each kind. That way I'd be able to check later if Frankenbug ate any or not. I put the top of his cage back on and went to dinner.

As soon as I came back I counted up all the bugs. The little ones were hard to spot— except the aphids, that is. They were holding perfectly still while the ants stroked them on the back with their antennae. The aphids squirted out a drop of sugary honey-dew in return.

Six, seven, eight . . . eight aphids. Two of the aphids were missing! I leaped off the floor and shouted, "Frankenbug ate some-thing!"

"What?" called my mom from the kitchen.

"Nothing," I answered, and sat back down to watch this with my very own eyes.

But then, after a minute or so, I realized that I'd jumped for joy too soon. It wasn't Frankenbug who ate the aphids. The ground beetles did it. One of them started munching on another aphid right before my eyes. I'd totally forgotten that ground beetles are carnivores. And they must have been hungry after hibernating all that time.

As for Frankenbug, he was just watching all the bugs skitter and hop around in there. Once one of the weevils even crawled up and sat in between Frankenbug's antennae. But he didn't mind at all. He even looked amused, like he was enjoying the company.

But I wasn't amused. I was getting desperate. I looked up at Clyde the hawkmoth caterpillar in the terrarium on my shelf.

Clyde was never meant to be a caterpillar. He should have been born as a pig. Clyde was still chomping away on leaves even though he should have turned into a cocoon two months ago. Birch, catalpa, and weeping willow were his favorites.

Of course, most caterpillars eat a lot to store up energy for pupation. But not Clyde. He ate only for pleasure. Maybe, somehow, he knew that once he burrowed into the soil and pupated, he'd have to give it all up.

Anyway, Clyde had to be about the plumpest and juiciest three-inch morsel in the world. I doubted even Frankenbug could resist him.

"Clyde, old buddy," I said, getting the terrarium down off the shelf, "I really hate to do this. But you see, it's for a good cause. Do you have any last requests?"

Clyde was too busy chewing to answer.

"Of course," I said. "As if I couldn't guess."

I crawled out my window and jumped over the fence into Mrs. Rosekrantz's yard. Luckily it was already dark, so her poodle was inside the house and didn't yap as I picked off some leaves from her weeping willow tree. They'd already turned yellow in the autumn weather, but I knew Clyde wouldn't mind. Weeping willow salad was his favorite, no matter what color.

When I got back to my room I chopped up the leaves with my pocket knife and gave Clyde one last meal. Then I lifted him out of the terrarium, stroked him on the abdomen a few times, and slowly lowered him into Frankenbug's cage.

What happened next caught me totally by surprise. For the first few seconds Frankenbug and Clyde didn't notice each other. Then, all at once, they both reared up and froze.

Frankenbug's thorax was nearly straight up with his pincers pulled back against his body, kind of like a spooked horse who'd just seen a snake. And in fact, that's just what Frankenbug thought he'd seen. For now, as I took a closer look at Clyde, I saw a side of him that I'd never noticed before. Clyde wasn't rearing up his head. He was rearing up his rear end, and there, on his underside, was a stunning sight: the eyes and mouth of a ferocious snake. The hawk-moth caterpillar startle display! How could I have forgotten?

Actually, with Clyde it was pretty easy. He wasn't exactly the type to go around startling his enemies. He was too busy eating. Come to think of it, Clyde didn't *have* any enemies. His only cagemate was Eddie the snail, and Eddie wouldn't give Clyde the time of day.

A whole minute went by. Neither of them budged. I reached in with a pencil and scooted Clyde around a little so Frankenbug could see that he was just a normal caterpillar, not really a snake. It didn't help. Clyde kept flipping his snake head back up, and that's all Frankenbug could see. (Actually I was kind of proud of Clyde. I had no idea he could get that far off the ground.)

Things were at a standstill. After a few minutes I started to worry that Frankenbug might get a leg cramp. So I carefully reached in, picked Clyde up out of the cage, and put him back in his terrarium.

Frankenbug returned to normal pretty quickly after that, but I think Clyde was a bit shaken up. He stared at his weeping willow salad for a while, but didn't eat any more of it, and he pupated that very night.

chapter

By Saturday Frankenbug was starting to look bony, or, what I mean is, bonier than usual. It was time for some drastic action.

I waited until my mom went out shopping, then headed straight into the kitchen and got some of every single kind of food he might like: a slice of roast beef, a drumstick, a hot dog, a piece of pepperoni pizza, a banana (peeled), coconut custard pie, a dill pickle, black olives (pitted), an eggplant slice (Eddie's favorite), oatmeal cookies, and every other leftover I could find.

I got out a big silver tray from my mom's china cabinet, put all the food on it, and set it on the kitchen table. Then I brought in Frankenbug's cage and put it next to the tray.

I'd never picked Frankenbug up since he'd come alive, but now I had no choice. It felt like picking up a lobster, except for the wing cases and curled-up scorpion tail. The stinger on the end was less than an inch from my hand, but luckily Frankenbug didn't use it. Gently I set him on the kitchen table next to the tray of food.

"C'mon, Frankenbug, eat something!" I pleaded. But he just sat there.

I knew what the problem was. The food wasn't moving, just like before. So I cleared the salt and pepper shakers off the lazy Susan and put the tray of food on top of it. Then I started spinning it around in front of his face.

Now he perked up a bit, and his head swiveled back and forth as he watched the different foods go by.

Then, suddenly, he lifted himself up. I slowed the lazy Susan, staring with awe as Frankenbug reached out with his front legs and scooted himself forward. It was just an inch or so, but he was crawling! He scooted forward again, and again. Soon he was right in front of the lazy Susan.

I stopped spinning it and my breath stopped too, waiting to see what would happen. Frankenbug lifted his pincers over the edge and then, with one big push, boosted himself up on the tray.

It was bumpy up there, but Frankenbug started crawling anyway. He was after something—but just what, I couldn't tell. He climbed over the coconut custard pie and the black olives—of course, I thought, a true carnivore would never bother with those. And sure enough, now he was headed for the roast beef! Nope—he scooted right over it. It must have been too well done for him.

Next Frankenbug crept onto the slice of pepperoni pizza. This could be it, especially since so many of his parts sounded like Italian food. But soon I could tell he wasn't interested in the pizza either—he was just stepping across it. Then, halfway over, he got one of his hind feet stuck in the mozzarella cheese.

Frankenbug started tugging his leg. I held my breath again, not knowing if the spider-silk stitches were going to hold. Of course I still had some extra silk in case of emergencies. But now I wished I'd double-stitched those leg joints.

Frankenbug tugged and tugged, and finally, with one big heave, he pulled his leg loose. From the cheese I mean.

But now there was a bright red slice of pepperoni stuck to his back claw, and Frankenbug didn't like it. He lifted his leg up, cocked his tibia back like a miniature catapult, and fired. The pepperoni slice sailed through the air and stuck on the kitchen wall with a splat. It was the first real sign of Frankenbug's strength.

He took a few more steps and then, with a sudden jolt, he stopped. Frankenbug was stalking his prey. He crouched down and held perfectly still. I waited to see which piece of food would be his victim. Ever so slightly, his abdomen began to sway back and forth—just like a cat before it pounces. Frankenbug was getting ready for the attack.

All at once he lurched forward with his pincers open and grabbed something big and white. It was a marshmallow. The big, puffy kind you roast over the campfire.

He raised the marshmallow to his mouth and ripped it open with his jaws. I ran to the kitchen cabinet to get the whole bag. By the time I turned around the marshmallow was gone. I put another on the tray, and then another. He ate four without stopping. I fed him the last one right out of my hand.

At last—Frankenbug was eating. But . . . marshmallows? Where had I gone wrong?

I went back to my insect books to look for an answer. It turned out that the goliath beetle isn't exactly the Goliath I'd thought. He's a giant all right—six inches long and heavy as a rat—but he's not a carnivore. His favorite food is the oozy, sweet sap of trees. Marshmallows are sweet too and made from the roots of mallow plants. That explained it. Frankenbug had a sweet tooth. Actually a sweet mandible.

This wasn't the greatest news. But maybe there was still time to teach him to be a carnivore while he was young. After all, he still had the *brain* of a carnivore, even if he didn't have the stomach of one. If I could just get him to taste one little bug, everything might come back to him.

I wasn't sure how, though, until one morning at breakfast. I got an idea from the frosted flakes.

After school that day I brought Frankenbug's cage into the kitchen and picked out some weevils and crickets. I put them in a dish, poured on some maple syrup, and set it on the table. Then I picked Frankenbug out of the cage and placed him right in front of the dish. He ignored it.

"Please, Frankenbug, just one little bite," I urged. "You can't live on marshmallows alone. This is good for you—it's *nutritious*." I was starting to sound like my mom.

He just stared at me. He probably didn't know what "nutritious" meant.

I got a silver spoon out of the drawer, poured on some syrup, and held it up to Frankenbug's mouth. He eyed it for a moment. Then, for the first time in his life, he started to uncoil his vampire moth proboscis.

It was an inch-and-a-half long and took a while to straighten out, but it finally did. I held the spoonful of syrup next to the barbed tip. Frankenbug dipped it in like a straw.

After a minute or so I pulled the spoon away, because I didn't want him to lose his appetite. Then I put the dish of syrupy weevils and crickets right in front of him again.

This time he noticed them. He leaned over the rim of the dish, right above a fat, juicy weevil. I thought this could be the big moment. *Attack!* I yelled in my mind, *Attack!* But all Frankenbug did was suck up the syrup.

Next I heated some fudge sauce on the stove. I dipped in the weevils and crickets one by one with the cooking tongs and let them cool on a plate. They looked delicious. I even wanted to try one myself. But all Frankenbug did was nibble off the chocolate coating. What a waste of those doodlebug mandibles.

It was no use. Frankenbug just wasn't meant to be a carnivore. The next day I stopped by the drugstore on the way home from school and bought some jelly beans, shoestring licorice, caramel chews, and a pack of bubble gum for myself. He liked it all, but he got his mandibles stuck on the caramel. I had to pull him loose.

Frankenbug wanted to try my gum too. I could tell by the way he kept staring at my mouth while I was chewing it, almost like he was stalking his prey. But of course, if he got stuck on caramel, I couldn't take a chance with gum. I stopped chewing it in front of him because I didn't want to make him envious, and also, to tell you the truth, because I was a little bit afraid he might try to snatch it out of my mouth.

So that proved it. When it came to sweets, Frankenbug wasn't fussy at all. He *always* had room for more.

Sweets or not, of course, I was happy that Frankenbug was finally eating. But I was also wondering: Would a marshmallow-eater be fierce enough to protect me from Jeb McCallister? The more I studied my insect books, the more I doubted it. I found out that goliath beetles are so friendly that African children keep them as pets!

And now I had to admit that Frankenbug was friendly too, not the monster I'd planned him to be. Come to think of it, Dr. Frankenstein's monster wasn't really a monster in the beginning either. The only reason he became one is that everyone was too afraid of him to help him. Even Dr. Frankenstein ran away from him. If you ask me, he was more of a monster for doing that than the monster himself.

I decided to change Frankenbug's name. It just didn't fit anymore, so I started calling him Frankie instead. I also decided to let him roam around free in my room. The other bugs weren't in any danger, since Frankie wouldn't hurt a flea.

Even though Frankie wasn't a monster, I wasn't giving up hope that he might protect me from Jeb. After all, he still had all those weapons—maybe I could teach him how to use them. But first I had to teach him basic things like jumping and flying.

chapter

Looking at Frankie's body, I didn't think it was going to be easy. He'd been eating about twelve marshmallows a day for three weeks, plus different kinds of candy on the side, and he was starting to bulge out in places. So late one night I sneaked in and weighed him on the kitchen scale. He was over one pound. Now I was seriously wondering whether Frankie might be too heavy to get off the ground.

But I didn't think it was impossible. Lots of bugs are like that—their bodies look too big for their wings to lift. Mr. Simmons said bumblebees are too heavy to fly according to the laws of physics, but they just break those laws and fly anyway. So Frankie could just break them too. At least enough to fly around and attack the bully if necessary.

But to make things a little easier for him, I decided to put Frankie on a diet. Only six marshmallows a day, and no candy. That seemed to work okay, and he started losing weight, about half an ounce a week.

After a month of dieting it was time to start Frankie's flight training. Not outside, of course—it was still only January, with lots of snow on the ground. Until spring came, we could practice in my room. Not flying, of course, but jumping—the crucial first part of a good takeoff.

Actually it wasn't as hard as I thought it would be. All I did was put a marshmallow on my shoulder and stand in the middle of my room. After about five minutes of staring at it, Frankie suddenly sprang to my shoulder. But he sprang a little too hard and flipped over backward onto the floor. I guess he didn't know his own strength.

After that I taught him to jump to my shoulder whenever I tapped my finger there.

Then I fed him a marshmallow right out of my hand. We practiced that trick all during the winter.

Finally March came and the snow melted. It was time to go outside. There was always a chance Frankie might try to fly away, but I didn't think he really would. After all, marshmallows don't grow on trees. And if Frankie was ever going to protect me from Jeb, he had to get used to being outdoors.

The first Saturday in March was too cold, the next one rainy. But the third Saturday was just right, a bright blue morning with no clouds, and that's when I took Frankie out into my backyard for the first time. He trembled a little in the fresh air. I gave him a tour of the trees and honeysuckle bushes and the Caterpillar Café, and we sat down in the grass to wait for the sun to warm up his wing muscles. Frankie sipped on some dewdrops with his vampire proboscis. Then it was time to start.

"Okay, Frankie," I said, "it's time to break the laws of physics." I carried him to the middle of the yard.

"Fly, Frankie," I said, bouncing him in my hands a little.

To my surprise, he didn't hesitate. He crouched down, squeezed my palms with his claws, and jumped into the air. The problem was, once he got there, his wings didn't come out, and he flopped to the ground. We tried the same thing a couple more times, but he plopped right down again.

Then I noticed something. Frankie was trying to fly, but he didn't know he had to open his wing cases first. I tugged at them a little, but I was afraid to pull too hard.

I put him down on a lawn chair, leaned forward, and lifted my arms out to both sides. "Like this," I said. He watched me but still didn't try it. My arms didn't look like wing cases at all. I needed a real beetle to show him how.

Luckily I found one in the bushes, a ladybug. He was small, I realized, but at least he had all the right equipment. It wasn't easy getting him to use it, though. I carried him over in my hand to the lawn chair, and as soon as he saw Frankie he rolled over on his back and played dead. That's how ladybugs defend themselves. Aside from tasting bad. But I kept turning him right-side up and nudging him with my finger. Finally he swung out his wing cases and took off.

Frankie was watching everything, but I wanted to make sure he really got it. I grabbed the ladybug in midair and made him take off from my hand three more times.

Then it was Frankie's turn. I held him up in my palms in the middle of the yard again. This time he opened his wing cases and stretched out his wings to the side. Compared to the ladybug he looked like a jumbo jet.

His wings started to vibrate. They made a deep buzzing noise, kind of like jet engines warming up. Frankie was getting ready for takeoff.

He perked up his antennae to test the air currents. Next he cocked his hind legs back and dug his claws into my hands to get a firm grip. Then into the air he leaped, beating his wings in an invisible, buzzing flurry. Frankie was airborne!

At first he was going almost straight up, with his abdomen hanging low, and he looked more like a helicopter than a jet. But then he managed to pick up speed and level out. The problem was he couldn't steer. Frankie held his pincers up for balance, but he was still wobbly in the air and before I knew it he was headed right for the elm tree.

"Watch out, Frankie!" I yelled, but he bumped into the trunk and tumbled head over tail to the ground. Luckily he wasn't hurt, just a little dazed.

I decided to point him away from the trees on takeoff. That helped a little, but now the problem was landing. About half the time Frankie landed upside down. At first I ran over and turned him right-side up, but then I thought I shouldn't pamper him. What if he did that when I wasn't around?

So the next time it happened I watched to see if Frankie could flip back over by himself. After waving his legs in the air for a minute, he started pushing against the ground with his scorpion tail—two, three, four times, and then, with one big snap, he jackknifed back up.

He flew a few more times after that, but I could tell Frankie was getting tired, so I took him inside.

While he was asleep I went into the living room, with the buzz of his wings still in my ears, and found the pitch on the piano. It was an F (F for Frankie!), which meant, according to a chart Mr. Simmons gave me, that Frankie's wings were beating 352 times a second. That was slower than a mosquito, which flaps 600 times a second, but faster than a honeybee or a dragonfly. Not bad for a homemade monster bug.

The next morning we went out and practiced some more. Frankie's wings glinted blue and gold in the sunshine, and even though he wasn't up to thirty-five miles an hour yet, he still could fly back and forth and even hover a little, just like a dragonfly. He started making a big circle around the trees, landing on my shoulder each time. Then, right in the middle of his tenth circle, he suddenly flew up to a high branch of the sycamore, folded his wings back, and gazed out over the treetops.

"Frankie!" I called. But he didn't come.

This was the moment I'd been afraid of. I raised my hand to my shoulder and tapped three times. Frankie looked at me and gazed back out over the trees. Then he opened his wings and took off. He glided across the backyard, looped behind me, and landed on my shoulder. I gave him a marshmallow.

We went outside almost every day after that. Sometimes I took him for walks in the woods, but mostly we played in my backyard. On sunny days I even let him stay there while I was at school. I left a dish of marshmallows for him under the bushes. It was usually empty by the time I got home.

But one morning in early April he didn't stay there. I was halfway to school when all of a sudden I felt him land on my shoulder. I knew those claws anywhere.

"What are you doing here, Frankie?" I scolded. "You've got to go back home!"

I nudged him off, but he just flew up to a nearby branch and sat there, watching me. I pointed in the direction of my house.

"Go!" I said. But Frankie didn't budge. So I just kept walking down the sidewalk. He flitted back down to my shoulder.

"Frankie, you can't come with me," I said in a serious voice, and prodded him off again. He started following me from branch to branch. That was okay, but what about while I was in school? What if he landed on my shoulder during recess?

Luckily he didn't. I spotted him again in the trees as I was walking home after school. When I got to Ash Street I tapped on my shoulder, and he whirred down for a perfect landing.

From then on he followed me to school every morning and home again every afternoon. What I worried about most was that someone would notice him and try to catch him. Especially with those colors of his.

One day a girl in my class named Mary Wolcraft told me that she'd seen this huMONgous bug in the trees when she was walking to school. She said it looked pretty rare and that I should try to catch it. I told her she must have seen a bird.

"Well," she said, "it was colorful like a bird—about as colorful as a peacock—but it had big mandibles and antennae too!"

I wanted to say he wasn't as colorful as a peacock, but I stopped myself. "Oh," I said instead. "In that case, I'll have a look after school."

That was a close call, but most of the time Frankie was good at keeping out of sight. And now that I thought about it, he was doing exactly what I'd planned for him to do: following me at a distance, but staying close enough to protect me from any bully. Of course, I still didn't know if he'd actually help me when I needed him to. I'd never seen Frankie use his weapons on *anything* except marshmallows and chewy candy. He was even afraid of a tubby caterpillar. So how could I be sure he'd defend me from Jeb McCallister?

chapter

10

Meanwhile the science fair at my school was scheduled for early May, and I planned to do a bug project as usual. I could have entered Frankie, but that was out of the question. So it would have to be a different kind of bug.

In third grade my project was titled "The Millipede Myth." I counted the legs of 20 millipedes I caught in the woods and found that the average was only 178—not even close to 1,000.

In fourth grade my project was on earthworm charming. It's kind of like snake charming, only the worms start out in soil instead of a basket, and you don't have to use a flute. I experimented with different kinds of music at home using my mom's cassette tape player, and found that Beethoven's Fifth Symphony worked best. For some reason, though, on the day of the fair it didn't work at all, even when I turned up the tape player full blast. So I got a sixth grader, Rodney Metzlebaum, to bring his trumpet into the auditorium and play whatever he knew, which worked really well.

Anyway, that was soil bug projects two years in a row, so I decided to do an aquatic bug this time—water striders. My project was to show how they walk on water. The secret is in the way they spread their weight out over their long, spindly legs, and it doesn't hurt to have hairy, waterproof pads on your feet, either.

For my display I made a poster and brought in some live water striders that I caught in the creek in the woods. I put them in an aquarium and let people look at them through a magnifying glass. I explained how their claws are up a ways on their legs so they won't poke through the skin of the water. And I dropped some midges and mosquito wrigglers in the tank to show how the water striders grab them with their front legs, stab them with their beaks, and suck them dry.

It was a good day except for what happened after school. I was walking home with my water striders and leftover mosquito wrigglers in a big gallon jar. I wanted to keep them for a few more days in my room before I let them go.

But Jeb was waiting for me halfway home, the same place he'd waited when I brought home the moon moth. He was just standing there on the sidewalk, snapping his gum, blocking my way.

"Hey Bugbrain," he said. "Fancy meeting you here."

"Yeah," I said, keeping my head down.

"Whoa there—just a minute," said Jeb, stepping in front of me. "Whatta ya got in the jar?"

"Nothing," I answered.

"Oh yeah? Then why are you holding it up like that?"

I looked at him. "You already know."

"Uh-uh," said Jeb. "We can't all be geniuses around here, Bugbrain."

"Water striders," I muttered.

"Water spiders?"

"Water *striders*. Bugs that walk on water."

"Lemme see," said Jeb.

I shook my head. "No way."

Jeb gripped my arm and yanked the jar out of my hands. Then he stepped back, grinning and unscrewing the metal lid.

"They walk on water, huh? Well, how 'bout concrete?" The lid clanged to the sidewalk.

"Don't do that, Jeb!" I yelled, grabbing for the jar. He elbowed me away.

"Just a little experiment, Bugbrain. Now, let's see—what should my hypothesis be?" He put his finger to the side of his forehead, pretending to think. "Oh yeah—I've got it! My hypothesis is that water striders *can't* walk on concrete. And here, Bugbrain, is my method."

Jeb raised the jar with both hands and slowly poured the water on the sidewalk. The water striders hit the concrete hard and just lay there, stunned from the fall.

"Well, looks like the results are in, doesn't it?" He smirked, flinging the jar to the grass.

I ran at Jeb with my fists clenched and threw a punch straight in his face. He blocked it with his arm and slugged the wind right out of my stomach. I doubled over and fell to the ground.

"Now, now, Bugbrain. You don't want to get in the way of scientific progress, do you?" Jeb glared down at the water striders on the sidewalk. "Just for that, I'm afraid I'm going to have to put these specimens out of their misery."

Jeb pulled the gum out of his mouth, hawked up a big wad of spit, and spat right on top of them. Then he raised his foot up and smashed it down on the water striders one by one, twisting his shoe into the sidewalk each time.

"That'll teach you to mess with my experiments," he grumbled, and started to walk away.

But then, somewhere from high up in the trees, there came a deep buzzing sound. A chain saw? I looked at Jeb. He seemed confused.

"What's that noise?" he asked. We both turned and saw him in the sky. It was

Frankie—no, not Frankie. Frankenbug. Zooming toward Jeb at full speed.

Jeb took a step back. "What is that thing?" he asked. "Why's it coming toward us?"

I looked straight at him. "Not *us*, Jeb. *You*."

Jeb wheeled around and took off down the sidewalk, but he didn't get far. Frankenbug was closing in on him, with his pincers out and tail high, and when Jeb looked back over his shoulder he suddenly tripped and fell smack on his face. Frankenbug buzzed down next to his ear.

"Help! Get him away!" Jeb choked, his cheek pressed to the concrete.

"Okay! Just hold still!" I answered, watching to see what Frankenbug would do next.

He circled back up and hovered in midair, like he was taking aim. Then all at once he dived, engines roaring like a fighter bomber, straight for his target.

Faster and faster Frankenbug dived, his wings and weapons shining like steel in the sunlight, and now I saw that this amazing, patchwork creature I'd put together in my own room, this creature who lived on marshmallows and was scared of pudgy caterpillars, was now just moments away from zapping the enemy and proving himself a fearless hero.

But then something went wrong. Just a few feet above his target, Frankenbug suddenly wobbled out of control, did a triple aerial cartwheel with a reverse twist, and flopped upside down on top of Jeb's back.

"AAAARHHHGH!" yowled Jeb, his whole body stiffening. He stared at me, eyes bulging like gumballs, and hissed: "What's it doing?"

"I'm not sure," I answered, trying to sound urgent, "but it's got its stinger right next to your skin, so I wouldn't move if I were you!"

In fact Frankie was still sprawled upside down on Jeb's back, with his legs wiggling wildly in the air.

Hurry, Frankie, I thought at him. Flip over—you can do it!

He must have gotten my message, because a moment later he stopped waving his legs and started snapping his tail against Jeb's back.

Jeb glared at me frantically.

"DON'T MOVE," I shouted, pushing my hands at him. "DON'T MOVE—WHATEVER YOU DO!" But inside I yelled, MOVE, FRANKIE, MOVE!

Then, like a miracle, he did. With one big jerk of his tail, Frankie sprang up and landed on all sixes. He riffled his wings back into place and started to creep up Jeb's back.

"YAAAAAAAHHG," Jeb wailed. "Can I shake it off?"

"No way!" I said. "He'll sting you if you do!"

Jeb let out a long, low moan as Frankie crept across his shoulders and paused a few seconds, his antennae quivering. Then he crawled back down Jeb's back and perched himself on Jeb's rear end.

"Hurry, Frankie!" I thought. "That's the target. Now do something—before it's too late!"

Frankie did something all right. He started cleaning his pincers.

I thought it was all over then. Jeb would heave him off and squash him any second.

My only hope now was to rescue Frankie before he did.

But then, with a quick swivel of his head, Frankie put down his pincer and raised himself up on his legs a little.

That's when I saw it. There was a pack of baseball cards in Jeb's back pocket, with a big slab of bubble gum inside.

Frankie crept closer, his antennae trembling. He'd smelled the gum.

"What's it doing?!" asked Jeb. "Get a stick or something—I'm begging you!"

"Okay," I answered, "just hold still!"

Frankie reached down with his mandibles first, but the wrapper was too slippery. Then he lifted his right pincer up in the air and stretched the claws wide open.

Uh-oh, I thought.

In the next instant Frankie jammed his pincer straight down, grabbing and yanking on the gum with all his might. But he grabbed a lot more than the gum.

"YEEOOOOOOOOW!" shrieked Jeb. It was a pinch of steel, like none I'd ever seen. Then Jeb started writhing back and forth on the sidewalk, and Frankie couldn't keep his balance. In a flash he spread his wings and zipped off into the sky.

"I've been stung!" Jeb screamed, clutching his rear end. "Call an ambulance!"

I stepped over to him. "It didn't sting you, it only pinched you."

"Who cares! Call an ambulance!" he hollered again.

I didn't exactly want there to be an ambulance and a siren and all that, and, anyway, I knew Jeb didn't really need it. So I just walked up to the nearest house and pretended to ring the bell. After a minute or so Jeb hobbled up from the ground, so I went back over.

"Nobody home," I said.

"Never mind," he snarled, narrowing his eyes at me and chewing on his gum. "What do you think that thing was, Bugbrain?"

"Beats me," I shrugged.

"Oh yeah?" said Jeb, kicking a rock. "Why do you think it went for me and not you?"

"I really don't know."

"Well I don't know either, Bugbrain," Jeb said, lowering his voice and pointing his finger straight into my face. "But one thing I do know is, the next time that thing comes around, it *will* go for you—you can be sure of that." Then he limped off toward Juniper Street, mumbling cusswords I didn't even know existed.

After he was gone I went over to the water striders, but there was nothing I could do for them. So I just headed home.

Frankie did it! I thought as I hurried along the sidewalk. Not exactly the way I'd planned, with that topsy-turvy landing, the short break for pincer-cleaning, and a pinch-attack instead of a sting, but after all, even superheroes have their clumsy moments. All that mattered was that Frankie got the bully in the end. If you know what I mean.

chapter

Frankie wasn't in my backyard. He must be resting someplace, I figured, after using up so much energy—he had to come home soon. But he didn't. That night I sneaked out my bedroom window with my flashlight and checked the backyard about twenty times. I hardly slept at all.

The next morning I was back out at dawn, but still no Frankie. I ran up and down my street calling out his name, looking in all the trees and even in the neighbors' backyards. But no luck.

At school everyone was talking about the monster bug. They said Jeb's wound was so bad that he had to stay home in bed. Jeb's father, Police Chief McCallister, had put out an emergency warning to the whole town. And the police department was offering a hundred dollar reward to anyone who could bring in the monster bug, dead or alive.

It even made the front page of the morning newspaper, and Mr. Avery held it up in front of the whole class. The headline read

GIANT INSECT ATTACKS CHILD; POLICE ADVISE CAUTION

and underneath was an artist's drawing of Frankie based on how Jeb described him. It made him look like some kind of flying dragon.

"This is serious, people," said Mr. Avery. "We don't know yet just how dangerous this creature is, or even *what* it is. Meanwhile the school administration is recommending that you take the bus or get a ride home from school instead of walking. I myself have volunteered to stand guard during recess."

Some students raised their hands.

"Yes, Joseph?"

"Mr. Avery, what should we do if we see it—on the playground, I mean?"

Mr. Avery thought for a second. "Lie down on the ground and hold still."

"But, Mr. Avery, that's what Jeb did!" shouted Billy Markle.

"No talking out of turn, William," said Mr. Avery. Then he pointed to someone else. "Nicholas?"

"Mr. Avery, I was wondering—how are you going to guard the playground?"

Mr. Avery nodded and walked over to the supply closet. He pulled out the broom, lifted it up with both hands, and whisked it back and forth through the air a few times. "With this," he said, frowning like an anti-terrorist commando.

Somebody in the back of the room started cracking up and then coughed to cover it. Mr. Avery put the broom back in the closet and told us to open our science textbooks to page ninety-one.

At lunch I sat at the farthest corner of the table, under the basketball hoop. Actually that's where I usually sat anyway, but today I was afraid somebody might ask me about what happened. Lucky for me, though, no one seemed to know that I'd even been with Jeb the day before, and they didn't ask me anything. For a while at least.

"Just think, a real monster on the loose—in our town!"

"Yeah, this is definitely the coolest thing that's happened around here since the hailstorm last summer."

"Or the sonic boom that busted my living room window."

"That happened before you were born."

"So what!"

"I wonder where it came from."

"An F-104 Starfighter."

"No, squidbrain—I'm talking about the monster bug! And besides, it was an F-16 Fighting Falcon, not an F-104."

"Sounds screwy to me—this monster bug thing. I bet it's a fake."

"Jeb's just exaggerating."

"Yeah, he just wants the girls to feel sorry for him—poor wittle Jebby-webby poo!"

"And he wants to make sure no one thinks he was a wimp."

"What do you mean?"

"Think about it—big, bad Jeb McCallister, getting burned by a measly bug!"

"But they say his wound is really big— bigger than a snakebite. He even had to go to the hospital to have it checked."

"How could a bug do that?"

"Maybe it wasn't a bug."

Suddenly everyone got quiet and looked over at the person who said that. It was Aaron Lubovsky.

"Huh? What do you mean, Loobie?" somebody asked.

"Maybe it was an alien," said Aaron. He was holding a celery stick stuffed with peanut butter.

"Gimme a break!"

"C'mon Loobie, have you ever even seen an alien?"

"No."

"Then how do you know this is one?"

"Well," said Aaron, "didn't you ever notice? A lot of aliens in movies look like bugs."

95

"That's just because the movie-makers copy bug shapes!"

"It's an alien invasion!" hollered Billy Markle, diving under the cafeteria table.

"Take cover—here they come!" shouted Skipper Barton, squishing a glob of mashed potatoes on Billy's neck.

"Hey—cut it out! That's my new shirt!"

"Not anymore!"

"Just think, they'll have to cancel school—for a week at least," said somebody else.

"Maybe a month!"

"Lunkheads, if it's an alien invasion, there won't even *be* a school for us to go to. They'll *vaporize* it."

"That's even better!"

"Wait a minute—wait a minute," said Skipper Barton, holding up his hands to stop the conversation. "If this really is an alien invasion, then tell me—where's the flying saucer? I mean, these beings couldn't exactly zing in from outer space without a saucer! They'd get scorched!"

Quick as a wink Billy Markle grabbed the half-full applesauce dish from his plate and whooshed it through the air like a UFO toward Skipper. "Here it *izzzzzZZZZZZZ*" he hummed and plopped it upside down on Skipper's head.

"Hey, speaking of aliens, why not ask Buzz over there!"

Everyone at the table looked over at me. I was chewing on a Frito.

"What do you think it was, Buzz? An insect or an alien?" asked Nick Sanders.

"Yeah Buzz, what do you say?" joined in the others.

I finished chewing, swallowed my bite, and looked into their faces. "Definitely an alien," I said.

"How do you know?"

"Yeah, Cricketman—what makes you so sure?"

I shrugged my shoulders. "It takes one to know one," I said. A few guys laughed, a few groaned, and then the bell rang.

After that I thought I was home-free until the end of the day. But I was wrong.

Mr. Avery was writing long division problems on the blackboard when a sixth-grade girl with a bobbing ponytail walked in and handed him a piece of pink paper. Mr. Avery scrunched his eyebrows at it, then looked at me.

"Adam," he said in that serious voice of his. The bottom of my stomach fell out. Everyone knew what pink slips were: a ticket to the principal's office. Mr. Avery had even written a few of those himself, but never for me.

Now I could feel the whole class watching me as I headed out of the room.

"What'd you do wrong?" whispered Derek Hershman, who sat next to the door.

"I don't know," I whispered back, which was almost true, but not quite.

chapter

The principal, Mrs. Burgess, was talking to a secretary when I walked into the front office. She had sparkly gold earrings dangling from her ears, and she was smiling.

"Hello, Adam, please come in," she said cheerfully. She motioned me through the door of her office, and I saw Police Chief McCallister sitting there. He had on his tan, neatly ironed uniform, including a gun in his holster and a big silver badge pinned to the front of his hat. I swallowed.

"Have you met Chief McCallister before, Adam?" asked Mrs. Burgess.

"Um, no, I don't think so," I answered.

Chief McCallister stood up from the chair and reached out his hand.

"Hello, Adam," he said in a low rumble.

"Hello," I said, as my hand disappeared inside his.

"Jeb tells me that you two were walking home together when the monster bug attacked," said Chief McCallister.

I didn't answer.

"I know you must've been frightened," he continued. "But don't you worry, son. I've got half the police force working on this case. We'll be apprehending the monster bug very soon."

"I see," I said. There was a brief silence, and then Mrs. Burgess spoke.

"Would you like to thank Chief McCallister for his efforts, Adam?"

"Thank you, sir."

"Now, Adam," she continued, "the main reason I called you in today is that a counselor, Dr. Derrybinkle, has made a special visit to our school today, and he'd like to talk with you a little bit."

"But . . . why me?"

"Well, we thought you'd been through quite an . . . ordeal yesterday, and we just wanted to make sure you're handling everything okay."

Mrs. Burgess guided me into a little room next to her office.

There was a man in a dark suit and tie in there, sitting in a chair. He had a bald spot on top, wire-rimmed glasses, and brownish gray bristles on his chin.

"This is Dr. Derrybinkle, Adam," said Mrs. Burgess.

"Hello, Adam," said Dr. Derrybinkle. His voice was smooth as an oboe. "Please have a seat." He opened his hand toward the chair in front of his, and Mrs. Burgess hurried out of the room.

"Now then," he said, folding his hands in his lap. "How are you feeling today?"

"Fine," I said.

Dr. Derrybinkle just kept peering at me through his thick glasses, not blinking at all. This must be how a bug feels to be looked at under a magnifying glass, I thought. I squirmed.

Finally he spoke again. "Is that all?"

"Huh?" I asked.

"Is that the only feeling you're feeling right now? Fine, I mean."

I couldn't think of any more feelings right away, so I said the first one that came to mind.

"Umm . . . dandy."

"Excuse me?"

"Dandy. I'm feeling fine and dandy," I said.

"Oh, that's fine. I mean good. But, I wonder, do you by any chance feel some other feelings too, for example, upset . . . or worried?"

"Oh yeah, I'm a little worried."

The doctor nodded his head. "I can imagine that," he said. "After everything that's happened. Would you like to talk about it?"

"Okay," I said.

There was another pause. Then Dr. Derrybinkle said calmly, "You can say anything you want."

I fidgeted some more. "Um . . . like what?"

"Oh, like . . . how it feels . . . to feel worried."

"Um, well, I am kind of worried about the bug," I said.

"You mean . . . the monster bug?" said the doctor.

"Yeah, that one," I nodded.

"Oh, I can believe that. I once got stung by a bee when I was seven. It really hurt."

"Was it a honeybee or a bumblebee?" I asked.

Dr. Derrybinkle stared at me for a second. "I don't really remember," he said, smiling faintly. "I probably didn't know the difference."

"Honeybees leave their stinger in your skin," I said.

"Uh-huh. I see," said the doctor. He scratched behind his ear. "Anyway, getting back to the monster bug—I'm told that it's much bigger than a bee. And I guess you should know—you saw it, right?"

I nodded.

"And you saw it sting a classmate of yours, didn't you?"

"Pinch."

"Excuse me?"

"It only pinched him," I said.

"Okay—pinch," said Dr. Derrybinkle. "How did you feel, Adam, when you saw that?"

"Um . . . well . . . it's kind of hard to describe the feeling."

"Yes, I'm sure it must be," said Dr. Derrybinkle. "And you don't need to try, Adam, you don't need to try." He crossed his legs and wrapped his hands around his knee.

"Tell me, Adam, did you have any trouble sleeping last night?"

"Uh, yes, actually I did."

"Did you imagine the bug . . . coming after you?"

"Not exactly," I said. "But I did imagine him coming to my backyard."

"I see," said Dr. Derrybinkle. He picked up a pencil and notepad from the desk and rested it on his lap. "Did you try to protect yourself in some way—say, for instance, lock the window or hide under the covers?"

"No, actually I kept getting out of bed to check if he was there."

"You mean, you looked out the window?"

"No, I crawled out."

"Of the window?"

I nodded.

"Into your backyard?"

"Yes, with my flashlight."

Dr. Derrybinkle gazed at me for a moment, then blinked. It was his first blink since we'd started talking.

"I see," he said slowly, rubbing the bristles on his chin. "And what were you going to do . . . if you saw it?"

"I was going to hold him and pet him and feed him a marshmallow," I answered. Dr. Derrybinkle blinked again and jotted something down on his notepad.

Then he looked at his wristwatch and glanced at his briefcase on the floor. "Let's try something different now," he said, pulling out a stack of big cards.

"I have some pictures here, Adam, that I'd like you to take a look at." Dr. Derrybinkle lay the cards facedown on the desk.

"You may have made pictures like this in art class," he continued. "But today I'd like you to just look at these and tell me what you see."

"Like looking at clouds," I said.

Dr. Derrybinkle glanced up. "Yes, that's right. And there's no right or wrong answer to any of these. Just tell me the first thing that comes to mind."

"Okay." This was turning out to be more interesting than math class.

"Here's the first one," said Dr. Derrybinkle.

"That's a fog-drinking beetle of the Namib Desert," I said.

Dr. Derrybinkle started taking notes. "A fog-drinking beetle . . ." he repeated.

"Of the Namib Desert," I said. "It's in southwestern Africa."

"Right," he said. "Could you point to it for me?"

"Sure. Here's his head, his legs, and here's his rear end."

"Sticking up in back?"

"Yes. Facing the ocean."

"Ocean?"

"The Atlantic," I answered.

"Right. But . . . why is he facing it?" asked Dr. Derrybinkle.

"Well, there's no water on the desert, so he just waits for the fog to come in and condense on his back. Those are the little drops starting to form right there." I pointed.

"Why don't we go to the next one," he said, picking up another card.

"Those are two praying mantises mating," I said.

Dr. Derrybinkle didn't say a word, but he was still watching me. So I kept talking.

"Here's the female—she's the big one—and here's the male," I explained.

"Uh-huh," said Dr. Derrybinkle, turning the page of his notepad and scribbling down more notes.

"I see some movement in this picture," I said.

Dr. Derrybinkle stopped writing. "Oh?" he asked.

"Yes. She's biting his head off."

The doctor sat up a little, straightening the knot of his tie. "Well then, anything else for this card?"

I looked again. "There isn't room for anything else. It's a close-up."

"Hm-mmm. Why don't we go on." He lifted the next card up slowly.

I studied it. "That's either a German or

an Oriental cockroach head. I'm not sure which."

"I'm sure either will do," said the doctor. He wasn't taking notes anymore.

"Here's the antennae, here's the mouth, and here's the eyes—simple, and compound," I said, pointing to each part. "These sparkly things on his eyes are crystals, for hunting in the dark."

"Is that right." said Dr. Derrybinkle.

"But of course," I added, "this cockroach couldn't go hunting even if he wanted to."

He nodded. "So . . . I guess it's safe to say there's no movement in this picture."

"Oh no," I replied. "Cockroach heads can stay alive for twelve hours after decapitation. His antennae are still twitching. His palpi too."

"Palpi," said Dr. Derrybinkle.

"Yes. This cockroach is probably hungry, or what I mean is, he probably *thinks* he's hungry." I smiled.

"Hungry cockroach head," he said.

"Hm-mmm." I nodded.

Suddenly the doctor chuckled a little.

"Excuse me, Adam. And uh . . . let's see— what do you suppose this hungry cockroach head would like to eat? If he still had a stomach, that is."

"Well, scientists have discovered that cockroaches' favorite food is glazed cinnamon rolls," I answered. "Aside from that, they're very fond of boiled potatoes and bananas dipped in beer."

"Fascinating," said Dr. Derrybinkle. "I'll be sure not to leave any of those out in the kitchen." He looked at his watch. "Well, Adam, that's all we have time for today. I want to thank you for taking time to talk with me."

"You're welcome."

Dr. Derrybinkle gathered up the cards, put them back in his briefcase, and stood up.

"I think you had a rough experience yesterday, Adam, but you're going to be just fine. Get plenty of rest in the next week or two—kind of take it easy. You know, watch some TV, read some comics—anything but *Spider-man*, okay?" He winked.

"Okay," I said.

Dr. Derrybinkle patted me on the head and stepped out of the room. I hopped over and pressed my ear to the door.

"How is he, Doctor?" Mrs. Burgess asked.

"He'll be fine," replied Dr. Derrybinkle. "He's had a mild emotional trauma and right now he's making use of a psychological defense known as 'identifying with the aggressor.' That means, basically, that he imagines himself as a friend of the enemy—in this case, the monster bug."

"Why would he do that?" asked Mrs. Burgess.

"Well, if you're friends with the monster, then you won't be its next victim," explained Dr. Derrybinkle.

"I see," said Mrs. Burgess.

"The boy has a vivid imagination," continued the doctor, "and he's putting it to good use right now. But there's nothing to worry about—he'll get over it soon."

Mrs. Burgess thanked the doctor and saw him out the door. Then she let me out and sent me back to my classroom.

I took the long way back, past the auditorium and the music room, to give myself a chance to think about what Dr. Derrybinkle said. He got the part right about my being friends with the monster bug, that was for sure. But I wasn't imagining it all, and I wasn't going to get over it soon. Close, Dr. Derrybinkle, but no cigar.

During afternoon recess a lot of kids were looking up in the trees and over in the backyards past the playground fence to see if they could spot the monster bug. Some second-graders even made up a new game called "monster bug tag," and some third-grade girls made up a brand-new chant for jump rope:

> Monster buggy came to town,
> Scared the bully to the ground,
> Stung the bully's fat rear end.
> How many days did it take to mend?
> One, two, three, four, five . . .

Meanwhile Mr. Avery was trudging around with the broomstick slung up on his shoulder like a rifle, squinting back and forth at the sky. Once Skipper Barton and Billy Markle hid behind a big tree and cried "Help! Help! The monster bug!" and made Mr. Avery dash halfway across the playground to save them.

I don't know what happened next, though, because I was eavesdropping on a bunch of sixth-grade boys near the jungle gym. They were talking about forming a search party to hunt down the monster bug and get the reward. They planned to meet in the park after school. So on my way home I stopped and waited till they showed up. Then I spied on them from behind a tree.

There were about twenty of them altogether, and they came with butterfly nets, baseball bats, and cans of bug killer. For a while they just knocked at a Wiffle ball with their bats. Then they gathered around in a huddle, hooting and cackling and making plans with a stick in the dirt. They drew lines of all the main streets and split into three groups to try to search them all. Then they started arguing about how to divide the reward money.

I wanted to stop them, but what could I say? A hundred bucks was too much of a prize, and some of them were already bragging about how they were going to spend it. I knew the only thing I could do was find Frankie first.

chapter

13

As soon as I got home I went straight to my backyard, but still no Frankie. Where could he be? I thought of the places we'd been together, and then I remembered the woods. Frankie had to be there.

I decided to wait until dark. I didn't want anyone following me to the woods or noticing me when I brought Frankie home. But I couldn't wait too long. The woods aren't exactly the safest place for a bug at night. That's when the screech owls and brown bats and nighthawks come out hunting for food.

At dinner I couldn't eat a thing. My mom wanted to know more about what happened the day before, but before I could tell her much the doorbell rang, followed by some hurried knocking. My mom went to get it. It was one of the sixth-grade search parties.

"Mrs. Cricklestein, we're looking for the monster bug that attacked Jeb McCallister yesterday after school. Have you seen it?"

It was Charlie Beaumont from down the street. I used to chase zebra swallowtails and black beauties with him.

"No, I haven't, Charlie, but I hope you find it," answered my mom.

"May we check your backyard?" asked Charlie.

"*No!*" I shouted from the kitchen. But it was too late. They were already around the side of the house and through the gate, yelping and whooping like a band of warriors. I ran into the dining room and watched from the window, hoping that Frankie hadn't come back yet.

The search party fanned out all over the yard with their baseball bats and butterfly nets and cans of bug spray. Some of them were crouched down as if they thought the monster bug was going to attack any second. When a robin suddenly swooped down, three boys dived to the ground and covered their heads.

"That was just a bird, you wimps!" yelled Charlie.

"Hey, look at this!" hollered another. They all ran over to the bushes.

"What is it?"

"A dish of marshmallows!"

"What's that doing here?"

"Maybe it's to feed an animal or something."

"Yeah, sure. How many animals do you know that eat marshmallows?"

"Well, my cat likes 'em."

"I couldn't care less about your cat!"

"Hey, can *we* eat one of those?"

"Of course not, bonehead! What if they're poison or something?"

"C'mon, let's go!"

The search party ran over to the next house. I slumped back down at the table and stared at my dinner. I still hadn't eaten my tater tots and lima beans.

"They must not have found anything," said my mom.

"Yeah," I said.

"From everything I've heard and read in the paper, Adam, that bug sounds pretty dangerous. You were lucky not to get stung yesterday."

"Pinched."

"What?"

"He only pinched Jeb, he didn't sting him."

"Oh, well, whatever," said my mom. "In any case, I want you to promise to be careful when you play outside—until they find it, I mean."

"Okay, Mom," I said. "If you don't make me eat my lima beans."

"It's a deal." She smiled. "But how about some of those tater tots?"

I speared one with my fork and put it in my mouth.

"Oh, and I almost forgot," said my mom. "I got a call from Dr. Dinkleberry today."

"I think it's Derrybinkle," I said, crunching on the tater tot.

"Oh—right. Anyway, he said you should try to get some extra rest for the next few days. And try to get your mind off bugs for a while."

"That might not be too easy," I said, still chewing.

"I know, honey," she said, "but you need to try. The swimming pool's going to open up next weekend. Maybe you can go for a swim."

"I don't know," I said. "The chlorine's pretty strong."

"Oh, Adam," answered my mom, smiling and sighing at the same time.

I finished my tater tots and went to my room. I pretended to do homework for a while, and around eight o'clock I turned off my light and climbed under the covers with my clothes still on. I waited until my mom was watching television in the family room. Then I got my flashlight from the desk drawer, opened my bedroom window, and crawled out into the night.

The air was warm and the moon was bright and the crickets were still chirping as I headed down the sidewalk and across the field to the woods. I watched my shadow slip beside me over the tall grass, and I looked at my watch and counted. Thirty-five chirps in fifteen seconds. Thirty-five plus thirty-nine equals seventy-four. Seventy-four degrees tonight. Fahrenheit.

The woods were dark, as dark as a cave, and filled with the *scritchety-scratch-screaking* and *ing-inging-jingling* of a thousand invisible bugs—two thousand, five thousand, ten thousand or more—all playing like crazy, all together but alone, like a wild, nighttime symphony of the woods.

I switched on my flashlight and stepped inside, onto the narrow dirt path. My light didn't shine too far—I'd run down the batteries bringing Frankie to life. But it was still better than nothing, and as I walked along the path I stopped every now and then to point the light at the trees and bushes.

"Fraaaankieeeee," I shouted softly into the darkness. "Where aaaaare yooooou?" But the only answer was the *scritch-scritching* and *jing-jingling* in my ears.

I came to a fork in the path and turned right, in the direction of a small clearing deep in the woods where Frankie and I always played.

"Fraaaaankieeeee, oh Fraaaaankieeeee . . ."

Then, from somewhere off the path behind me, I heard a different sound, a scuffling sound—like footsteps.

Fwisssht—fwisssht;
Fwisssht—fwisssht.

I whirled around and stood still, cocking my ear at the darkness. Now the sound was gone, but there was a ripple of silence somewhere deep in the trees, as if the bugs had noticed it too, and were listening just like me.

"Who's there!?" I shouted.

But there was no answer. I pointed my flashlight deep into the shadows on both sides of the path, but I couldn't see a thing.

And then, a few moments later, the clatter of the crickets and katydids rose up again.

Maybe it was just an animal. A raccoon, maybe, or a deer—just a deer.

But then I heard it again—the sound—and it was louder now. I switched off my flashlight and held still. The sound stopped too. I started walking again, faster, almost running. The sound started up again:

Fwisssht—fwisssht;
Fwisssht—fwisssht.

It was following me. Something—or someone—was definitely on my trail.

I stopped and looked back at the path behind me, the path that could take me out of there right then, back across the field, back home to my bedroom.

No—not yet. I couldn't leave without making sure about Frankie. No matter what I had to check the clearing—and I had to get there soon.

All at once I remembered the shortcut across the creek. I knew where there was a secret log bridge, because I'm the one who laid it across. But getting there from here, in the dark—that I'd never tried.

I waited until the next bend in the path, then slipped through some bushes on my right, hurdled over a log, and hunched to the ground, listening. I didn't hear it now, the scuffling sound—only the screaking, scratching chorus of everything else. I peered through the darkness, listening for the bull-frogs in the creek to get my bearings. Then I moved ahead, staying low and treading as quietly as I could.

But it was no use. The dead leaves from last autumn rustled with every step. And to make things worse, now the crickets and katydids were quieting down for *me.*

I straightened up and dashed headlong through the trees, arms pumping, feet pounding over the dark blur of ground ahead of me. All I could hear now was my own breathing and the whipping and *thwak-cracking* of the branches at my side and under my feet. And the less I could hear of what was behind me, the faster I ran.

But then I broke through some bushes and jolted to a stop, teetering on the high, slippery edge of the creek. The moon lit up the water like a sliver of black light cutting through the forest.

I held my breath and listened. The chirruping of the crickets and katydids was back to normal, and I couldn't hear the scuffling anymore. Maybe I'd gotten away.

A hundred yards up I could see the log bridge over the water. I sidestepped my way along the steep clay bank, grasping at bushes and overhanging branches to keep from sliding down, and soon I was there.

The log was slick with dewy moss. I stepped out, holding my arms up for balance, and in three tottering steps I was across. I bounded off again, weaving and ducking my way past the branches and thickets. In less than a minute I reached the clearing.

"Frankie," I called softly. "Frankie? Are you there?"

I switched on my flashlight and pointed it around. A glint of flashy maroon caught my eye, and that's when I saw him, clinging to a low branch near the edge of the clearing.

"Frankie!" I shouted, and stepped toward him.

"Not so fast, Bugbrain!"

I spun on my heels, pushing the flashlight in front of me, and saw Jeb McCallister step out from behind some trees. He was carrying a huge, metal-rimmed net, the kind you catch fish with.

"What are *you* doing here?" I asked.

"No, Bugbrain," said Jeb, "the question is, what're *you* doing here?"

"But you're sick in bed!" I said, shifting sideways to hide Frankie from him.

"No way, man," he said, taking a step closer. "That was just an excuse to get out of school. I'm after the hundred bucks like everyone else, and it looks like I've come to the right place!"

"I don't think so. There's nothing here."

"And you're just taking a little stroll in the woods tonight, right?"

I stared into his face, lit up like a phantom in the flashlight's dim beam.

"Gimme that," said Jeb, jutting his chin toward the light.

I shook my head.

"What's the matter, man? I said gimme that, and I meant it!" Jeb wrenched the flashlight from my hand, then held me at arm's length while he swung it around in the darkness.

"Well, well, what have we here?" he said, spotting the tree Frankie was on. "A little monster bug resting on the branch? The vicious little monster bug that attacked me in cold blood?"

Jeb tossed the flashlight down, lifted his net up with both hands, and lowered his voice. "Well then, hold still, my little monster bug, because now it's my turn."

He took a step toward Frankie, then another, and in the next moment I rushed him with my shoulder, plunging hard into his side. But I didn't knock him down, and as soon as Jeb got his balance he grabbed me by the shirt and hurled me to the ground.

"Out of my way, twerp!" he yelled. Then he turned back toward Frankie.

"Fly, Frankie, fly!" I called out. But Frankie didn't fly, and I knew it was because his wing muscles were cold and there wasn't any sunshine to warm them up. Jeb stopped dead in his tracks.

"What'd you just say?" he asked, his eyes narrowing. "Did you just *talk* to that thing?"

I stared back at him.

"Are you trying to tell me, Bugbrain, that this is *your* bug?"

I didn't say a word.

"Oh man, Bugbrain," said Jeb. "You're in for it now—in for it really bad." He shook his head. "I should have known it all along. This is *your* bug, isn't it?"

I looked over at Frankie, then back at those dark, jeering eyes. "Yes," I said.

Jeb spat hard on the ground, wiped his mouth with his sleeve, and poked his finger at me. "Well lemme tell you something, Bugbrain. My old man is heaping mad about this bug, and once he knows it's yours, he'll throw you in jail!" And then, with one big sweep, he raised the net and scooped Frankie off the branch.

"Gotcha!" he yelled.

"Frankie!" I shouted.

"It's no use, Bugbrain. He's all mine now—all mine." Jeb bunched the net together and held it out. Frankie was trapped in the bottom, not moving at all.

"You know why I used a fishing net instead of a baseball bat?" he asked.

I shook my head.

"So I can torture him first, that's why!" Jeb pulled a cigarette lighter out of his pocket. He flicked it on and moved the flame under Frankie's tail.

"Your pincers, Frankie!" I cried. "Use your pincers!" But Frankie still didn't move. I sprang up and made a lunge for the net, but Jeb shoved the lighter right in front of me.

"One more step, Bugbrain," he snarled through the flickering light, "and you'll burn too!"

I stared into the flame, only inches from my face, and held still. But in the next moment, out of the corner of my eye, I saw a shudder in the net. I didn't turn my head or even move my eyes, but I could see them now, the giant pincers of the African emperor, reaching out in the darkness. They'd always been black before, but tonight, in the middle of this clearing in the moonlight, those pincers had an eerie, bluish green glow.

I looked into Jeb's eyes.

"You wouldn't really burn me," I said.

"Oh yeah?" he scowled, the flame dancing in his dark pupils. "Why don't you just try something and see?"

The pincers clamped down on the net and cut through it with a single snap. Frankie slipped out and clumped to the ground.

Jeb glared at him, sucking in a furious breath. Before I could move he raised his foot up behind Frankie and slammed it down. But Jeb's foot hit bare dirt, and now Frankie was on my shoulder. He'd jumped up, with his wetapunga kickers, faster than my eyes could see.

Frankie gripped me tight as I reeled around and leaped for the path. I dashed ahead with reckless strides, pumping hard with my right hand and holding Frankie on my shoulder with my left. A second later I heard the *scrush-scrush-scrush* of Jeb's footsteps behind me, gaining fast, and I kept my eyes on the fork ahead, thirty yards . . . twenty yards . . . ten yards, and now Jeb's breathing was in my ears, his feet pounding closer and closer. I jammed in my heel and cut right, arming away the branches and bouncing off each step to keep from stumbling on the roots and rocks. It was too noisy to hear Jeb now, to know if he was one yard behind me or ten, and I didn't look back, didn't dare, for a hundred yards or more. Then, from somewhere deep in the trees, I heard a burst of cursing and the words, calling through the darkness: "You can't escape, Bugbrain! The cops'll be after you now!"

I didn't stop running but I slowed enough to dodge the branches instead of crashing through them.

"We lost him, Frankie!" I whispered between breaths. Frankie still had his eyes straight ahead and his claws fixed tight on my shoulder. He wasn't used to this kind of excitement. It was time to get him back.

But where? Jeb was right—he'd tell his father everything and the cops would probably come to my house that very night. I decided to hide in the museum, in the insect room. I had my key with me, and they wouldn't look there, at least until morning.

I turned left at the next fork and curved around to the creek. It was way downstream from the bridge, so all I could do was grab a jutting root and slide into the water. In two steps I was in over my knees, with my shoes sunk deep in the silt. I slogged across, still not wanting to slow down, and on the other side I lifted Frankie up first and then pulled my way up.

This part of the woods I didn't know well, but I still had my bearings and it was just a few minutes before I came out onto a field near Culver Street, about three blocks from the museum. I cut straight across the field, then stayed in the shadows of the lawns the rest of the way to the museum.

It was all closed up and dark when we got there. I hid behind some evergreen bushes next to the building to catch my breath, and to make sure no one had followed me. Not a soul.

"That was a great getaway, Frankie, really great," I said, lowering him from my shoulder. "Those scorpion pincers came in handy again, didn't they? And those wetapunga kickers too."

Frankie turned his head toward me, and I looked into his eyes. They were a deep, glimmering purple now—the color praying mantises' eyes turn at night to see better in the dark.

I nestled him in my arm and crept around the side of the museum to the insect room. I opened the door with my key and locked it again from the inside. It was dark in there, and I'd left my flashlight back in the woods. So I lowered the window shades and switched on the lamp on Mr. Simmons's desk.

I made a bed for Frankie in an empty terrarium, but he wouldn't get inside. So I let him sleep on Mr. Simmons's desk instead. Then I got a blanket out of the closet for myself, turned off the lamp, and lay down on the floor. We spent the night with the insects, all quiet behind the glass.

chapter

14

Mr. Simmons nudged me awake the next morning. He said the police were searching all over town for me and that my mom was worried to a frazzle. I showed him Frankie and told him the whole story about how I'd made him and brought him to life. I told him why Frankie had attacked Jeb. And I asked Mr. Simmons to help me save him. Then there was a loud knock on the door.

"Who is it?" said Mr. Simmons.

"This is Police Chief McCallister. Open up, please."

Mr. Simmons glanced at my eyes, then stepped over and cracked open the door.

"Hello, Mr. Simmons," grumbled Chief McCallister's voice. "We're looking for a young man named Adam Cricklestein. Have you seen him?"

"Why yes, I have," said Mr. Simmons. "Is something the matter?"

"Listen, Mr. Simmons," said Chief McCallister. "The boy isn't in trouble with the law. We only want the bug. It's a menace to the community and has to be destroyed immediately."

Mr. Simmons pulled the door open a little more, and Chief McCallister stepped inside. Jeb was right behind him, holding a net in one hand and a big steel cage in the other, the kind dogcatchers use to catch stray dogs. Outside I could hear a group of guys from school riding up on their bikes.

"Who got the hundred bucks?" someone shouted.

"Jeb did!"

"Dang!"

Jeb grinned at me. "The exterminator's here too," he said. "He's got a whole tank of bug spray."

"Where's the bug, son?" asked Chief McCallister.

"Bug?" I said.

Jeb pointed to the desk. "There it is, Dad!"

Chief McCallister looked over at Frankie. "Great jumping grasshoppers," he mumbled, and reached for the net.

"Move back, everybody, this could be dangerous!" he warned, motioning us away.

But we just stood there, watching. Chief McCallister circled around the desk and stepped up behind Frankie, quietly, almost on his tiptoes. Then he lifted the net high up in the air and began to lower it. Frankie cocked his back legs.

"Gotcha!" shouted the chief as he thwacked the net onto the desk. But the net was empty.

"That's funny." Chief McCallister raised the net and flipped it over. "I could have sworn I had it." He glanced around the room. "Now—where'd that varmint go?"

"Up there, Dad—look!" said Jeb, pointing up at Mr. Simmons's bookshelf. Frankie was peering down from the top shelf.

"Well I'll be a son of a gun," muttered Chief McCallister. He climbed up on Mr. Simmons's swivel chair and reached the net out toward Frankie. But by now Frankie had his wings unfolded and humming, and as soon as the net got close he whizzed past Chief McCallister's ear.

"Whoa!" he shouted, grasping at one of the shelves to keep from falling backward. Then he swiveled himself around and gazed up. Frankie was whirring in the air above his nose.

Chief McCallister's face stiffened, and he hesitated a moment. Then, slowly raising the net to his side, he lashed out at Frankie with a giant *SWOOOSII.*

But Frankie just darted away and left the chief swirling around on the chair like a top. He bent over to slow himself, climbed back down to the floor, and spotted Frankie hovering in the corner above the cicada display.

"I've got you now," he growled, tromping steadily toward the corner. He stooped beside the moth meter for a few seconds, eyes squinting in concentration, then stormed forward with another lunging *whiii-isssh* of the net. But Frankie zinged over his head to the whirligig section.

Now the chief's face was red and his neck muscles were rippling at the collar. He bounded down the aisle, grunting and slinging the net back and forth through the air. Frankie swooped to the left, then to the right—always flitting just beyond the net's reach, like he was playing a game of tag.

"Dagblast it!" yelled Chief McCallister finally, leaning up against the bumblebee display case.

"Want me to try, Dad?" asked Jeb.

"No, son," he puffed, "this isn't child's play." Then he turned to us, straightening his hat. "As you can see, Mr. Simmons, this bug is resisting my best efforts. I'm afraid I'm going to have to resort to a different tactic."

Chief McCallister unhooked the billy club from his belt, fastened it onto his wrist, and looked up. "Now, where is it?" he asked.

Mr. Simmons and I just watched, our lips sealed.

"Um . . . Dad?" said Jeb, wincing.

"Yes?"

"It's—it's on your head, Dad."

"What?" muttered the chief, suddenly freezing. "What do you mean?"

"It's sitting on your hat, Dad, and . . . now it's unwinding its poker up there, Dad! Right on top of your hat!"

It was true. Frankie was perched on Chief McCallister's hat, slowly uncoiling his vampire moth proboscis. I couldn't understand why he would do that until I noticed his eyes. They were fixed on the chief's silver badge.

Of course. Frankie thought it was a silver spoon, the same kind I fed him maple syrup with.

"Get him, Dad!" shouted Jeb.

Chief McCallister glared at Jeb, looked down at the billy club in his hand, and glared at Jeb again. Then, without the slightest movement, he shifted his eyes over to Mr. Simmons.

"Could you . . . do something?" he murmured.

Mr. Simmons looked at me. "Adam, would you like to help Chief McCallister?"

I nodded, walked over, and raised my hand up to his hat. "C'mon down, Frankie. It's not what you think it is up there."

Frankie curled up his proboscis and crawled onto my hand. I clutched him in my arms and stepped back to Mr. Simmons.

Chief McCallister lifted off his hat and wiped his face with a handkerchief. "Jeb," he called, keeping his eyes on me, "bring me the cage."

"Sure thing, Dad." Jeb smirked as he walked across the room with the cage. Chief McCallister opened the top and stepped over to me.

"Put it in, son," he said. "Enough is enough."

I shielded Frankie with my arm and backed up against the wall. "He didn't do anything wrong!" I blurted out. "The only laws he broke were the laws of physics!"

For a few moments Chief McCallister just stared at me, puzzled. Then he spoke again. "Son," he said firmly, "I'm sure you don't want to get into any trouble yourself. But you've already pushed your luck by not telling me everything you knew yesterday in the principal's office. And if you persist now in speaking that way to an officer of the law, I assure you that you'll be in more trouble than you ever imagined. Now put the bug in the cage."

"Just a minute, please," said Mr. Simmons, taking a step forward. "As the museum entomologist, I should have some say in this matter."

Chief McCallister shot an annoyed glance at Mr. Simmons and set the cage on the floor. "Keep it brief," he said gruffly.

Just then there was a knock on the door, and in barged the group of guys, mostly Jeb's friends and sixth-graders from the search party.

"Where is it?" someone whispered to Jeb.

"Holy moly! Look at that thing!"

They all stared at Frankie in my arms, then fell silent in Chief McCallister's stony gaze.

"I understand your concern about safety, Chief," said Mr. Simmons. "However, I must inform you that I have carefully examined this insect and have concluded that it poses no danger whatsoever."

"No danger?" asked Chief McCallister.

"That's correct," said Mr. Simmons. "In general, aside from the common housefly, which doesn't bite but can spread disease, insects posing the biggest threat to humans are predators such as kissing bugs, assassin bugs, mosquitoes, and lice, which survive by piercing the skin of their victim and sucking its blood. This bug we see here," said Mr. Simmons, motioning to Frankie, "despite its . . . unusual size, is not a predator at all."

I'd never heard Mr. Simmons talk like this before, but it sounded good.

"Oh no? Not a predator, you say?" Chief McCallister scowled. "Then what about that mouth of his? It looks like an artillery unit!"

Mr. Simmons glanced at Frankie's mouth. "I agree it looks a bit . . . bellicose. But the animal kingdom is filled with curious, overblown shapes and structures that seem to go well beyond the function they serve. The tail feathers of peacocks are a good example, or the antlers of Irish elks."

"Or the antlers of stag beetles!" I added.

Chief McCallister breathed out heavily. "Well, that's all fine and good, Mr. Simmons," he said. "But we're not talking about peacocks or Irish elks right now. We're talking about monster bugs." He pointed at Frankie in my arms. "What's your proof? How can you be so sure this thing isn't a predator?"

Mr. Simmons nodded. "The main proof is in this insect's diet. It doesn't eat meat."

"Well, Mr. Simmons," huffed the chief, "if it doesn't eat meat, then just what *does* it eat?"

Mr. Simmons paused a moment, then answered in a calm voice. "Marshmallows."

Chief McCallister's eyebrows squeezed into a frown. "Did you say . . . marshmallows? You mean the kind you cook over the campfire?"

"That's right," said Mr. Simmons.

"But he likes them plain," I said.

Chief McCallister ignored me again, pointing at Frankie's mouth. "It needs all of that, uh . . . equipment, just to eat a marshmallow?"

Mr. Simmons nodded, picked a marshmallow out of the bag on the desk, and held it up to demonstrate. "We haven't studied the matter carefully yet, but it seems that the fluffy viscosity and cylindrical shape of a marshmallow put special demands on an insect's mouthparts," he said, twirling his finger around the edge of the marshmallow. Chief McCallister was watching carefully, but he didn't say a word.

"Granted, this creature's mouth may not win any design awards," continued Mr. Simmons, "but from the standpoint of rugged, tooth-and-claw survival, it seems to function quite well." Frankie tugged the marshmallow out of Mr. Simmons's fingers and started nibbling on it.

Chief McCallister grunted and folded his arms across his chest. "Well, that sounds quite logical, Mr. Simmons, but if you recall, approximately five minutes ago this so-called marshmallow-eater of yours uncurled his ... uh ... doohickey on top of my head. Now I'm no expert, but I do know what those doohickeys are for. Are you trying to suggest, Mr. Simmons, that this bug thought my head was a marshmallow?"

Mr. Simmons paused. I could tell he was stumped.

"No," I broke in. "He thought your badge was a spoon!"

This time Chief McCallister didn't ignore me. "That will be quite enough from you, son," he said.

Then Mr. Simmons spoke up. "What Adam meant to say, I think, is that this insect's choice of landing sites had to do with foraging behavior, not aggression."

"Not aggression?" boomed Chief McCallister. "Then how, Mr. Simmons, would you describe this bug's behavior the day before yesterday, when, at approximately 3:25 P.M., in the vicinity of Cedar Street, it brutally attacked my son on the way home from school?"

"That behavior," replied Mr. Simmons, "was purely an act of defense."

"What do you mean?" asked the chief.

"Why don't you ask your son what I mean?" said Mr. Simmons.

Chief McCallister looked over at Jeb. "Well, Jeb?"

Jeb bulged his eyes out with surprise. "I don't know what he's talking about, Dad! I was just minding my own business, like always!"

Chief McCallister turned back to Mr. Simmons. "Well?"

Mr. Simmons looked at me. "Adam?"

I looked up at the chief. "Jeb . . . squashed my science fair bugs on the sidewalk. Water striders—about ten of them."

"No way!" said Jeb. "We were just walking home from school together!"

Chief McCallister nodded. "It seems we have some conflicting testimony here, Mr. Simmons. Unless there were some witnesses that afternoon," he said, glancing at the crowd of kids, "I have no choice but to take my son's word on this."

"I didn't see it myself," spoke up Evan Brewster, one of Jeb's friends, "but Jeb wouldn't ever do anything like that!"

"Yeah, he and Adam are buddies!"

Chief McCallister picked up the cage. "Let's have the bug, son. *Now.*"

"Excuse me," came a voice from the group of kids. It was a girl's voice. I looked over and saw Mary Wolcraft stepping up from the back, the same girl who'd spotted Frankie in the tree that time.

"I didn't see Adam and Jeb that afternoon, but I did see something else," she said.

"Oh?" said Chief McCallister. "And what might that be?"

"I saw the squashed bugs on the sidewalk."

"That doesn't mean a thing, Dad!" broke in Jeb. "They could've been anybody's bugs!"

"Maybe so," said Mary. "But they were definitely water striders."

"How could you tell, young lady?" asked Chief McCallister.

"Because of their long, skinny legs," answered Mary.

"So what!" said Jeb. "Spiders have long legs too!"

"Yes, except that spiders have eight legs," said Mary calmly. "These had only six."

"She's lying, Dad!" said Jeb, shaking his head. "There's no *way* she could've counted the legs on those bugs. They were smashed to *bits!*"

A hush came over the room. All eyes watched as the color drained from Jeb's face.

"Thank you, young lady," said Chief McCallister finally. He frowned at Jeb and lowered his voice.

"You go back home now and wait till I get there."

And then, for one brief moment, Jeb showed a face I'd never seen before, a face that reminded me of any other boy I knew. It was just like when Clyde the hawkmoth caterpillar put his scary snake-head down— the one on his rear end—and then you could see his real face on the other side. You could see that he was just a normal caterpillar.

Jeb slunk to the door, sneaking a nasty glare at me as he went, but I didn't feel a thing. Chief McCallister turned back to Mr. Simmons.

"I have one more question for you," he said. "What if this bug is a pest? The local farmers are concerned about possible damage to their crops and orchards."

"As long as they don't grow any marshmallow plants," replied Mr. Simmons, "there should be no problem."

Chief McCallister nodded for a second, then stopped and eyed Mr. Simmons. "Just what kind of bug is this, anyway?" he asked.

"A very rare one, I think," said Mr. Simmons. "I'd like to keep it here in the museum for further study."

Chief McCallister heaved a sigh. "All right," he said. "But if anything happens, Mr. Simmons, I'm going to hold you personally responsible."

"I understand," said Mr. Simmons calmly.

Then the chief left the museum, followed by the group of kids. Mary Wolcraft was the last one out.

"Did you *really* count the legs on those water striders?" I quietly asked her.

"I didn't need to," she answered. "The mosquito wrigglers gave it away."

"Thanks," I said.

"You're welcome." She smiled.

chapter

Now it's June and Frankie loves the hot weather. I got to bring him home after everything calmed down, and now he darts and spins and soars around my backyard like he owns the place. Once a green darner dragonfly flew into the yard and Frankie chased him right back out. I've never seen a green darner give up a territory fight so quickly.

Frankie and I play inside the house a lot too. Now that my mom knows about him he doesn't have to hide in my bedroom anymore. She lets him come anywhere in the house except the kitchen at mealtimes. That seems pretty reasonable.

My mom was kind of upset with me for keeping Frankie a secret, but she admitted that she might not have let me raise him if she'd known about him, let alone create him in the first place. Now she calls Frankie by name and treats him like part of the family. She even buys marshmallows for him when she goes shopping. She still won't hold him though—that's going to take some time, I think.

Since I brought Frankie home, kids from my school have been coming over almost every day to see him, including some I've never met before. If they're not too scared I let them feed Frankie a marshmallow on their shoulder. Sometimes they bring treats for him too, like gummy bears, Milk Duds, sour watermelon slices, Atomic Fireballs, candy corn, and even some homemade fudge balls. I keep it all in a big jar in my room.

Frankie can't eat everything, of course, especially the jawbreakers and the ones with caramel. But he stares at the jar a lot.

Mary Wolcraft was the first person I invited over to meet Frankie. She likes bugs too and isn't afraid to hold him at all. Mary's curious about how I made Frankie and brought him to life, and she wants to see the trick with the flashlight and the lightning bugs. I told her it probably wouldn't work with the kind of lightning bugs around here, *Photinus pyralis,* but she wants to try anyway. So one of these evenings we'll catch as many as we can and give it a try, but I'm not planning to bring any new creatures to life, at least for the time being.

Now Frankie's favorite time of day is in the afternoon when the popsicle truck comes. As soon as he hears the music *ting-a-linging* down the street he zips over the roof of my house and lands on top of the truck. The first time he did that the popsicle man ran halfway down the street. But now he's used to Frankie and even knows his favorite flavor—grape. That's mine too. Of course, Frankie couldn't eat cherry even if he wanted to. Bugs can't see red. Purple is no problem.

I always hold my own popsicle in one hand and Frankie's in the other. Then he perches on my arm to eat his. The first time I gave him one he was so excited he grabbed it with his pincer and chopped it right in half. The top part fell on the ground, but of course Frankie still ate it. If you're a bug, you don't mind eating off the ground.

Anyway, that was a few weeks ago. Now Frankie's much better at eating his popsicle from my hand. Sometimes he sucks at it with his proboscis, and sometimes he just chews the ice.

Come to think of it, that's what I do too.